What Love

Looks Like

What Love Looks Like

* * * * * *

Kurt Bensworth

PHC Publishing
California

PHC Publishing
California

Contact us at PHCpublishing@cox.net

Printed in the United States of America

First Edition: August 2009

PHC Publishing is a division of Pacific Holding Company, LLC. The PHC Publishing name and logo is a trademark of Pacific Holding Company, LLC.

ISBN   978-0-9824547-5-6   2009903825

Jacket design by Austin Ranson
Jacket original artwork by Michael Godard

This book is dedicated to my wife and family.
What a remarkable adventure this has been.

To you, that part of me which I couldn't forget.

Acknowledgments

To the many who had contributed to the writing of this book, I give you a heartfelt thank you. They include two incredibly talented editors, Mia Taylor and Faith Black, and two unbelievably patient and intelligent copy editors, Christy Flamenbaum and Flo Selfman. Also, a special tribute to Michael Godard, who was willing to take a chance on me, without whose support, the book may never have been published. And I couldn't forget Nick Landis; your sage advice led us down a different path. Thank you!

To Tom Berean, Michelle Brych, LeAnn Hunt, Regina Lamb, Cathy MacAloney, Shannon Marzalek, Lynn Mitchell, Denise Pagett, Jeff Pajak, Cindy Reynolds, Kerry Rosenbaum, Courtney Silver . . . I'm thankful for your thoughts and insight.

Of course, I have to thank the most important person in my life—my wife. We've been married for twenty years and you're still my best friend. Thank you for not complaining about my 2:00 a.m. writing binges, or my insidious desire for perfection. Even as broken as I am, you continue to love me. How lucky can a man be?

Prologue

A lifetime past . . .

Last night I awoke from another one of those dreams. My life has changed significantly since we last saw each other. Although we have not spoken or kept in touch, she frequently visits me at night and in the early morning hours—certainly more often than I would like—to the point that I feel haunted by my own dreams. Time after time, I awake feeling as if I have left something unfinished, undone . . . empty. It's the feeling you get when your mind goes blank trying to respond to a question you know the answer to—it's right on the tip of your tongue, but then, nothing. There is a void where the answer used to be. After last night's dream, it is no different.

I STOOD IN a room somehow unfamiliar to me. It was small and cluttered with antiques. A grandfather clock towered in the corner, ready to strike one o'clock. Tiny porcelain figurines posed in a glass cabinet as if on display for sale. Precariously positioned in the middle of the room was a small, round pub table, absent of its chairs. On the table was an old-fashioned lace doily cradling a fluted glass vase containing a single rose—white.

A woman stood with her back to me. It was her mother.

I approached and asked, "Is Opal here?"

As if she were paralyzed, she did not turn around.

"Opal's not here," she said.

"I just saw her last night," I persisted. "She gave me her phone number, and I lost it. I purposely put it in this pocket to keep it safe and now it's gone."

"Well, I don't have it," she replied angrily, as she continued to address me without turning around. "And if I did have her number, I wouldn't give it to you!"

"Why? What have I done?"

"You've already done too much. . . . Besides, do you really think you were the one?"

With that, I awoke.

THE DREAMS ARE always different. I long ago quit trying to figure out what they meant. But I do wonder why I continue to have these unrelenting thoughts of her.

Something as simple as a song on the radio can trigger one of those memories. When I hear certain old love songs, like Bread's "Diary" or just about any song from The Carpenters, I immediately return to the days of *us*. Sometimes the feeling is so heartrending, the recollection so vivid, that I lunge to change the station. But the hardest song to listen to is Art Garfunkel's "Disney Girls." That was our song. The lyrics speak of happy times, a young man in love with a local girl, and a forever wife.

For me, the song represents a time of innocence and the raw emotions of first love. Since my last move, the dreams have increased threefold. Perhaps the change of address spurred some internal unrest. I recently moved into my dream home on Lake Mission Viejo, and life is good. Mission Viejo is a medium-sized city in Orange County, California, and prides itself on being one of the safest in the country. Mission Viejo is to Orange County what Bel Air is to Los Angeles, boasting one of the highest per-household incomes in the U.S. This largely Republican community embraces the many gated neighborhoods speckled throughout the city. I live on a large, lakefront property, in a two-story, six-thousand-square-foot contemporary house that includes four bedrooms, maid's quarters, billiard room, office, and a kitchen any professional chef would envy. The dock and accompanying ElectraCraft boat complete the picture.

When I was a boy, I never imagined I might end up living like this. Although only a few miles from where I grew up, this place might as well have been on another planet.

Moving has given me the opportunity to sift through several years' worth of accumulated junk. I threw out that twenty-year-old ratty baseball glove, trashed the used rags spotted with varnish, as well as the ten-key calculator missing the number nine button. The biggest mound was the give-away pile, made up of clothes that were too small or just plain hideous—green and yellow pants I couldn't squeeze into—and a hodgepodge collection of shirts much too repulsive and undersized to wear. I did keep a bobble-head hula girl that had been a gift from my Grandpa Heil.

Many of the boxes I hadn't seen in years, but there was one I had never lost track of. It was my private box—better known as the box where I stored things away for memory's sake, much like other people who keep photo albums as a way to keep their past alive.

In my case, this container is actually a wooden box that originally housed two bottles of Syrah from the Sonoma Vineyards. The wine was a gift from a man I later came to call Father, who, for my twenty-first birthday, introduced me to the pleasures of wine on a visit to the Sonoma-Napa Valley region. The wine is long gone, replaced by selected memories of a lifetime.

Because of last night's dream I decided to seek out the box. Sitting comfortably in my office chair, I slide back the wooden top from its frame, revealing an assortment of items: old love letters, cards, a used cologne bottle, a Batmobile Hot Wheels toy still sealed in its original packaging, newspaper articles, a little black book, and even a diary I kept on my first travels in Europe. There is an array of foreign coins, and at the bottom, wedged amongst some old photos, a small, dark green jewelry box. I know what's in it but choose not to open it.

Instead, I keep searching and feel my heart thump harder with the anticipation of unearthing a particular piece of the past. Usually I ignore the memories, but after the latest dream, I am ready to confront the past, to touch it, hold it, at least for a little while. Is it still here? Then I see it.

Without hesitation, I open the envelope, simply addressed "Kent Huffman," in her flowery handwriting, and remove the card. It is unpretentious and corny, even for its day. It depicts a couple standing on a beach, embracing, the ocean rolling in behind them as the sun sets. Above the couple, the card reads:

"As ever-changing as the sea,
As lovely as a melody,
Full of warmth and delight,
Mysterious, gentle as the night . . . is love."

Inside the card it continues:

"Always the same,
Yet ever new . . .
My love for you."

Then in her own writing:

"I have found love in You . . .
Forever . . ."
Opal

I savor the memory. It was the first time anyone had ever said "I love you" to me. Whenever I smell the smoke of an open fire, it brings me back to that night on the beach.

As I place the card back into its envelope, I come across three pictures of Opal I had overlooked. The first was taken on the Oregon coast during one of her many family camping trips. She sits alone on a hillside amongst dried weeds and cattails. Smiling as usual, her cherub cheeks greet the camera with an innocent, infectious giddiness. She is wearing denim overalls and a white sweatshirt, suggesting that even in the height of summer, the Oregon coastline can be rather chilly. Opal had given me the picture as a gift.

The second one is of the two of us in front of my childhood home. It was taken before one of the many school dances we attended. I have long, white-blond hair down to my shoulders, evocative of my surfer days. I'm dressed in a white and blue tux with bell-bottom pants. She wears an elaborate, light blue dress with a lace panel front that accentuates her budding young figure. At six foot one I tower over her tiny, five-foot-two, ninety-two-pound frame. Our arms are wrapped around each other as if we are the only two people in the world. You can tell I was happy.

The last picture is of her alone on the beach, ocean and sand in the background. Her long blonde hair is parted in the middle, the right side pulled behind her ear, the left hanging down across her cheek and brushing her tan chest. Her smile is bewitching, making you want to smile with her. You can barely see her eyes as she squints in the strong mid-afternoon sun. She was happy then.

I have a sudden powerful urge to look up. My eyes are drawn to my office wall, where a painting by Michael Godard hangs. I examine it more closely. The round cheeks, the blonde hair framing her face, the angelic portrayal—complete with angelwing peeking out behind her right shoulder—My god, it's her! It's Opal. I shake my head in disbelief. How could I not have noticed before?

I originally bought the painting at an estate sale three years ago because I saw in it eternal hope in the midst of tragedy and strife. It is the portrait of a young girl, long blonde hair flowing in the wind; several out-of-place gray strands imply she has been through a turbulent time. Her eyes are a brilliant shade of light blue, her lips small and delicate. She holds a dying, burgundy-colored rose with several of its dried leaves blowing in the wind. Apart from the sky, the withering rose, and her eyes, the painting is devoid of color.

Thinking back, I realize the dreams intensified soon after I bought the painting. I have dreamt of her ever since that day we made our promises. And for the most part, I have been able to ignore them. But over the past three years they have become increasingly potent, intoxicating, almost real. I have been at this crossroads many times before and have chosen to do nothing. This time, it will be different.

I need to find her. I have many questions. Through the years I have often wondered, "What if?"

Dreams . . .

Part I

Many years ago . . .

One

The penance of innocence . . .

It was a cool fall day, the air thick with the fog of an early morning marine layer, typical for Tustin, just a dozen miles inland from the Southern California coast.

Tustin was a medium-sized city of around 34,000 in those days, and although still dotted with working farms, it was already a growing suburb where families moved to escape the crowds and traffic of Los Angeles. It offered the comforts of big city life, yet within a short distance you could find a beach, a hilltop view of Orange County, or even watch farmers till their fields. The ravages of progress had not yet taken their toll on this burgeoning region. I was a junior at the city's namesake high school and felt every bit of the weight of my sixteen years on my shoulders.

The many who didn't know me, and even those close to me whom I called my friends, had no idea who I was or what I concealed. Outwardly, it looked like I had it all. California-handsome with long blond hair, sun-bleached to near white at times, skin tanned from my many surfing days, tall and lean, I attracted more than my fair share of attention. These good looks instilled in me a certain level of self-assurance, though some viewed this as standoffishness, even conceit. I knew it was all a façade. I had many secrets.

Of course, virtually everyone else in school was equally self-absorbed. Most couldn't see much past their own particular wants and needs. Thus, I felt safe from discovery—until her.

* * * * * *

IT WAS SADIE Hawkins week. Tustin was a modest community with a mix of blue-collar workers, farmers, and a fair number of wealthy families. Because of its farming history, Tustin High was big on the quaint custom of Sadie Hawkins week, when girls were given license to pursue boys, building up to Friday night's dance held in the gym. Yet, in spite of the golden opportunity, many girls couldn't summon the courage to ask out their closet crush, fearing the worst—rejection. For the boys it was a test, a way to compare their personalities and good looks against those of their peers, but mainly it was a true measure of one's popularity.

I had already been asked to the dance by a freshman, Meg, so I had a date if I wanted. I told her I would let her know by the end of the day, but I wasn't sure I wanted to go at all.

From her raised eyebrows I could tell she had been surprised by my response, and she walked away clearly disappointed. It wasn't that I didn't find her attractive; she was, in fact, quite pretty, and we would probably have a good time at the dance, but . . . I couldn't put my finger on it. It was more of a feeling than a reaction to anything she had said or done. Still, I felt apprehensive about her and, even more so, about the dance.

Walking through the school's main quad at noon was an adventure. There was always something going on. Whether it was the cheerleaders performing their routines, or the drama club putting on a skit, or some other guild raising money, the quad was constantly crowded with students. Today there was a row of three booths, each one representing a particular cause. The first, manned by two song leaders and the school's mascot, was selling T-shirts, sweatshirts, and other school paraphernalia on behalf of the boys' wrestling team. The next one was selling tickets for Friday night's dance, and the third booth, was, at first glance, staffed by three girls who were leaning over the wooden counter waving their arms and calling out to passing boys. A banner advertising "Kisses for 5¢" was thumbtacked to the back of the stand. Below the banner, held in place by Scotch tape, was a white poster board with large orange lettering reading "All funds go to the Sadie Hawkins dance decorating committee."

Then I saw her. In fact, there were not just three girls in the booth, but four. I hadn't noticed her at first, distracted as I was by the frantic pleas of the other girls. But suddenly out of the corner of my eye, I caught sight of a girl sitting quietly alone in the back of the booth, patiently waiting for a suitor to request her. She looked poised, back straight, legs crossed at the knees. Unlike her fellow volunteers, she looked straight ahead, not making eye contact with passersby. My curiosity was instantly aroused.

Who was this girl? I was certain I hadn't seen her before. I would have remembered. Keeping an inconspicuous distance, I watched her. And then she glanced in my direction, our eyes meeting for only the briefest moment before she turned away, as if embarrassed or shy. I kept on staring in the hope she would look back at me, but after thirty seconds or so, she still hadn't returned my gaze.

Shifting my focus, I saw she was dressed in the traditional Sadie Hawkins regalia, blue-jean overalls and a patchwork blouse. Her hair was parted in the middle, tied into two blonde ponytails by strips of the same fabric as her blouse. Her cheeks were heavily daubed with rouge and dotted with three large penciled-in freckles. Even from this distance, her large, light blue, oval-shaped eyes gave her a radiant look. She was beautiful, not in an obvious, overt way but more understated. She had the kind of beauty that, at first glance, might prompt you to think, "Well, she's cute enough," but then, if you really looked, "Wow" might be the best word to describe her.

I had to meet her. Brimming with confidence, I took a step toward the booth, and then the bell rang. Lunch hour was over and students rushed all around me, and before I knew it, she was gone.

I grabbed the first person I knew.

"Marc, who was in the kissing booth over there?" I asked.

"Sorry, man, didn't see any kissing booth. Why?"

I ignored him and pushed my way through to the booth. One of the girls remained behind, cleaning up a drink she had just spilled. Luckily, I recognized her.

"Gretchen," I said.

"Hey, Kent," she said, barely looking up as she continued to wipe up the mess with a napkin.

"Uh . . . who was that girl sitting with you guys?" I asked, gesturing to the empty chair.

"Oh, her . . . some sophomore," she said, appearing annoyed.

"You sound as if you're mad at her."

"I'm not. It's just, like, she didn't try very hard. She was friendly enough, but didn't bother helping us flag you guys down."

"So, who is she?" I could hear my voice rise with eagerness.

"Oh, I don't know, Opal somebody," she responded as she finished wiping up and then threw her cup away.

The bell rang again.

I had to get to class and this line of questioning was getting me nowhere.

"Thanks," I said. "See ya later."

One lesson I had learned my freshman year was the less said the better. I had seen too many of my friends lose relationships or ruin their reputations simply because they couldn't keep their mouths shut. In high school, rumors can destroy you, and one inquiry about Opal the sophomore kissing booth girl would be enough. Ask twice and a gossip column could start on me. I'd had my shot. I couldn't ask again.

Thought can change your perception, but not the reality of a lost opportunity.

Two

Spaghetti, Mom's specialty, was a treat for the whole family. She made it from tomato paste, spices, olives, tomatoes, and ground hamburger. Admittedly, to an Italian food enthusiast it might not have sounded authentic, but for us it was delicious and filling. It was rare for Mom to cook for the whole family. It meant her coming home early from work. Otherwise, she generally worked past six, and we were left to fend for ourselves. But this night everyone was home: Mom; my stepfather, Bernie; older sister, Keri Ann, whom I affectionately referred to as Sissy; and Danny, my younger brother. Even our eldest sister Mary, who never let us forget she was only our half sister, was there, though she lived a good fifteen minutes away in the city of Orange.

Sitting at the table and passing the food around, I felt comfortable and safe. Not long ago, my world had been very different. We spoke little as we ate, and that suited me just fine. I preferred to keep my thoughts to myself. Most of the time at school, and especially at home, I felt as if I didn't belong. I felt truly alone.

Mom, now on her third husband, had tried to make a home for us but made it acutely clear that it was all about her. I know in my heart she was well-intentioned as a parent, but being an only child herself, she might have been better off raising only one child instead of the four she was saddled with. Born on a farm in Iowa in the late 1930s, she grew up in abject poverty, a holdover from the Great Depression. Like Scarlett O'Hara, she vowed as a child that she would never go hungry again.

And it was true; we always had food on our plates, but our lifestyle fell well short of the mainstream middle class. From the outside, our house looked every bit the part—average and reasonably well-maintained. But beyond the front doors, it was sparsely decorated with furniture either awarded in prior divorces or hand-me-downs from Mom's parents, Grandma and Grandpa Heil. Between Mom's two divorces and Bernie's one, divorce had ravaged our family financially. Neither of Mom's prior husbands, Peter, Mary's father, nor Wes, Mom's second husband and the father of us three kids, had lived up to their child support obligations. Typically they paid late if at all. Like a house made of cards, one card toppling onto the next and bringing down the whole structure, our current stepfather, Bernie, followed suit in failing to pay child support for his three children. It's not that I didn't appreciate Mom and Bernie keeping a roof over our heads and clothes on our backs, but inside I wanted something more, to be more, maybe just a normal family.

Mom was a secretary for an insurance agency, not necessarily for the pay, which wasn't great, but mostly for the health insurance benefits and because the office was less than two miles from home, a five-minute trip.

Bernie was a day manager at a Coco's Bakery restaurant. He never complained about the long hours, the meager salary, or the forty-five-minute drive each way. He seemed genuinely happy. Of all the people in Mom's life, he was the one who loved her the most, and, as far as she was concerned, that was the way it had to be.

Bernie always sat at the head of the table. I took the chair at the opposite end, putting as much distance between us as possible, both literally and figuratively. Physically, Bernie was a large man, six feet tall and well over two hundred pounds, but not handsome. After his booming, deep voice, his eyebrows, or rather his one long eyebrow that stretched the width of his face, was the first thing you noticed about him. Coarse, wiry, and peppered with long gray strands, it was the ugliest damn unibrow I ever saw.

"Kent," Bernie said, "did you clean the garage like your mother asked?"

"No, I didn't have time today," I replied, between shoveling in a fork-load of spaghetti and a mouthful of bread.

"Figures," said Mary, from her place next to Bernie, under her breath.

"Shut up, Mary," I snapped. "You don't live here anymore, so you got nothing to say."

"Yeah, but I remember having to do all the cooking and cleaning for you kids when I did."

An astonished hush fell over the table.

"And when, exactly," Mom said, from her place on the other side of Bernie, putting down her fork, "are you supposed to have done all of this so-called cooking and cleaning?"

"Mom, when you were working . . . every night," Mary whined.

I sat back knowing full well what was coming next. Let the verbal sparring begin. We all thought Mary was nuts or at least delusional. She definitely had a few loose bolts floating around in her head. She would constantly come up with the most ridiculous, mind-boggling stories about things she had done, said, or witnessed, and seemed to believe every one of them whole-heartedly. Her compulsive lying was what had eventually led to her being kicked out three years earlier at eighteen. Mom could no longer handle Mary's shifting sense of reality. My relationship with her, if you could call it that, was one of barely maintained mutual tolerance. When she moved out, the house became a lot quieter.

After a few minutes of scathing exchanges, Bernie finally stepped in. "Now, Mary, let's settle down."

"Kent started it," Mary said. "He's the lazy shit, not me. You need to talk to him."

"Mom will. In the meantime, let's finish eating in peace."

Mary fumed.

Nothing was ever said to me. Bernie may have had this great big voice, strong and intimidating, but it was Mom who wore the pants. She'd shelved his balls long before their wedding night.

AFTER CLEARING AND drying the dishes, I sat down to do my homework on the same dining room table. Once I was done, I usually went for a walk to clear my mind. I never allowed anyone to accompany me. Grabbing a jacket, I announced loudly to no one in particular, "Going for a walk," and shut the door behind me.

Tonight, I looked forward to it more than usual, as I wanted to think about her. Although we had not exchanged a single word, I couldn't get the kissing booth girl out of my mind. For reasons I didn't understand, she intrigued me. I was impressed by the way she handled herself among some of the older, more popular girls, not yielding to the pressure to stand up, wave her arms, and generally make an ass of herself. Of course I couldn't forget what I had seen beneath the clownish Sadie Hawkins getup, an absolutely beautiful girl.

Across the street, my friend Scott's porch light was on, giving the impression they were home, although anyone familiar with their routine could assume if the porch light was the only light on, then almost certainly nobody was home. Scott was one of my best friends. His family was decent, honest, and well-off in comparison to other families I knew. Scott's father was a successful businessman and his mother a middle school teacher who taught piano lessons for spare cash a couple of days a week. Almost as a rite of passage, each of their three children was taught to play Bach, Clementi, and Mozart. Occasionally she would throw in a contemporary artist like Billy Joel or Elton John to keep their interest. Secretly, though, not one of them really enjoyed playing but accepted her instruction more out of a family obligation than anything else.

Directly behind Scott's house were the farm fields, my destination. Unfortunately, cutting through his backyard was out of the question tonight. There was nothing worse than getting caught going through someone else's property without permission. Besides, I knew his dad owned a gun, and I didn't like the idea of getting shot, even if I was sure no one was home.

I took the long route, walking up the street's slight incline to the corner and turning right. At about forty yards, the sidewalk gave way to a dirt footpath, marking the unofficial boundary between the residential area and the beginning of the Irvine farmlands. Turning right again and walking parallel to the backs of the houses, I kicked a few rocks, being careful to avoid the tractor tracks. I had learned in school that this type of road served two purposes: it was an access road for equipment and also acted as a physical barrier for weed control.

The farmland was owned and operated by the Irvine Company, one of the oldest and most respected in Orange County. In the 1860s, James Irvine I won the land in a lawsuit. Over the next twenty years, he accumulated over 110,000 acres, stretching twenty-three miles from the Pacific Ocean to the Santa Ana River.

Irvine died in 1886, and his son, James Irvine Jr., incorporated the Irvine Company in 1894. He shifted the ranch operations to field crops and olive and citrus orchards. Walking the path, I could go for hours without seeing a soul. This year they had rotated their corn crop to asparagus. I didn't mind; asparagus was short, giving me an unobstructed view of Irvine's city lights six miles away.

I stopped at my usual spot, an enormous, half-buried drainpipe measuring a good ten feet across. I sat on the end of it, swinging my feet in and out of its opening. Below me, a rocky, dry riverbed extended outward from the drainpipe's mouth. In the winter, runoff would pour through the pipe and onto the rocks, eventually settling into the sandy soil beneath.

The pipe's height offered a good view of the surrounding flat farmland.

I reached into my jacket pocket and pulled out a hard-pack of Marlboro reds that I had bought the week before. Flipping back the top, I chose a cigarette, placed it between my lips, and lit it. Every now and then I liked to have a smoke. It calmed my nerves, and tonight I felt oddly restless.

As I took another drag, the kissing booth girl popped into my mind. I knew I had come out here to think about her, but now I wasn't sure if that was such a good idea. Why bother? She didn't know who I was and I certainly didn't know her. Our eyes had met for a brief second, and now I couldn't get her out of my mind. Opal, that was her name. And what a beautiful name it was. Damn . . . she was a babe, too.

Who are you? I thought.

"Stop it," I said aloud as I exhaled the cigarette smoke.

Then it dawned on me. I had to meet this girl. Taking a last drag, I tossed the lit butt onto the rocks below and watched the sparks fly out like miniature fireworks. Popping in a Certs, I was confident my folks wouldn't detect the cigarette odor, at least not on my breath.

WHEN I GOT back to the house, my sister Sissy was making out with her boyfriend, Joe, on the front porch. I didn't like him.

Sissy and Joe were both seniors, and that was about the only thing they had in common. Sissy had a good reputation and was well-liked, even though she wasn't considered extremely popular. She was an above average student and generally had good common sense. Standing five foot one with brown hair and a freckled nose, she was adorable. Her biggest fault, as I saw it, was her insecurity, which gave her a need to be liked by everyone. Not that I didn't want to be liked too. I just had my own style—repression and distance worked well for me. Also, Sissy hated confrontation and tended to shy away from any type of disagreement. She meant the world to me, and most of the time I respected her wishes, but as in every sibling relationship, we had our share of arguments.

Joe was quite the opposite. He was what we called a "loadie." He smoked a lot of pot, and I hated seeing Sissy coming home stoned after being with him. He was loud, condescending, and considered himself a stud, despite standing barely five foot eight and weighing no more than a buck and a half. I thought he was a prick and detested the way he treated Sissy. Three or four times we had been within inches of coming to blows, and if it hadn't been for Sissy stepping in, I would gladly have drained him of his shitty attitude.

"Sissy, when you're done, can I speak with you?" I asked as I opened the front door.

"Hey, asswipe, she'll be in when I'm done," Joe said.

"Sure thing, dickhead," I replied casually. I could tell he was high by his bloodshot eyes.

"I'll let Mom and Bernie know your stoner friend's here," I said, shutting the door behind me. That would get rid of him soon enough.

On cue, Sissy came through the door right behind me. I was waiting, one hand leaning against the entryway wall.

"You don't have to be so mean to him. He's really a nice guy," she said.

"Oh come on, Sissy," I barked, "he's a pothead. You deserve better."

"Like *you've* never smoked it!"

"Yeah, but not every day. And I don't need it to know who I am."

"But I really like him."

"Then tell him to lay off me, or, I swear, next time I will lay him out. And you know I will, too."

"Don't be that way," Sissy said nervously.

"Just keep him away from m—" I was interrupted by a loud pounding at the front door. I beat Sissy to it and yanked it open.

"Shithead, step on out here," Joe demanded, as he backed away from the doorway, motioning by waving his hands that it was go time. He puffed out his chest, stood with his feet apart, and brought up his fists, trying to inflate his small stature.

"You sure you want to do this?" I asked, giving him a chance to back out, but hoping the answer was "yes."

"Oh yeah, come on, asswipe," he said, as he stepped farther back onto the lawn. He continued to hold his fists high, like he actually knew what he was doing.

Throwing off my jacket, I stepped outside and onto the edge of the dew-covered grass. I'd been in plenty of fights and knew I could take him. This was the moment I had been hoping for since the day I met him.

Joe lunged at me, swinging with an overhand right that missed badly. Behind me, I could hear Sissy yelling "Stop!" at top of her lungs. Ignoring her, I jabbed with a quick left, hitting him sharply in the right side of the ribs, followed by a right upper cut to the chin. Joe fell backward all the way to the sidewalk, nearly hitting his head. I took several steps toward him and was about to pounce when I saw Joe curl up into a fetal position, hands covering his face. Blood was flowing from the side of his mouth, staining the cement in an ever-widening red pool.

I was actually disappointed that it was all over so quickly. The ass-whooping had not lived up to my fantasies, but still I took pleasure in watching him moan in pain, like a cat in heat having no release. Sissy kept screaming something at me as she rushed to Joe's side, kneeling on the sidewalk and carefully picking up his head to cradle him in her arms.

"What is going on out here?" Bernie's thundering voice came from the doorway.

"Kent, in the house now! Keri Ann, tell your friend to go home. Both of you, let's go!"

Joe got up meekly, with Sissy's help, and hobbled to his car. They mumbled something to each other, she kissed him on the cheek, and he left. She gave me a dirty look as she passed me going into the house. Not exactly how I had thought the day would end, but satisfying nonetheless.

Or so I thought until I went inside . . .

Three

The good news was that Joe's parents decided not to sue us, unlike two years earlier, when I had broken another boy's jaw and his parents did sue for his hospital bills. Thankfully, the court had ruled in our favor, finding self-defense since the boy was three years older and had outweighed me by at least fifty pounds.

Joe, on the other hand, was technically an adult at eighteen and, having had the crap kicked out of him by a sixteen-year-old, didn't want any police involvement. I'm sure that wasn't his only reason either. He ended up making a trip to the hospital for stitches—three on the outside of his jaw and five inside his mouth, where one of his teeth had been driven straight through his lower lip. But the best news was that he was gone. Whatever happened between Sissy and him, I neither knew nor cared. I was just glad he hadn't called or shown up at our house. Perhaps Sissy had finally realized she deserved better.

Unfortunately, I did not get off scot-free. I got two weeks' restriction—one week for fighting and another for smoking. Apparently my smokes had dropped out of my jacket pocket when Mom picked it up after the fight. Normally, she would have turned a blind eye, but at that moment she chose to act as if she cared. Then there was Meg, who was ticked off at me as well. I had forgotten to tell her that I didn't want to go to the Sadie Hawkins dance. If I had been smarter, I would have just taken her. At least then we would still have been friends, and it might have given me an opportunity to speak to Opal, who was bound to have been there. But as it turned out, none of it mattered anyway. I was grounded.

* * * * * *

So, TWO WEEKS passed, and not once did I see Opal on campus or anywhere else. One would have thought that either by luck or pure coincidence I would run into her in a hallway, the quad area, the gym, or some other place at school. I began to think she no longer attended our school, and then . . .

ON THURSDAY AFTERNOON, the last bell of the day sounded as I stuffed my science and geometry books into my locker, pulled out my Spanish and health homework, and stashed them in my backpack. The light tan metal door of the locker squeaked as it closed. After making my way down the many corridors, I got to the main quad area. There she was, talking to my friend Aaron and another girl I didn't recognize.

She was even prettier than I remembered, especially without the Sadie Hawkins getup. Her blonde hair was long, past her shoulders, natural blonde, not like those from a bottle where you could see dark roots when the hair began to grow out. Thin braids started at each temple, and were tied together at the back of her head like Marcia Brady. Her eyes were a brilliant, light shade of blue, and she had sweet, ruby-red, Cupid's bow lips and the most alluring round cheeks.

She glanced in my direction and smiled at me. I smiled crookedly in return, but by then she had returned to her conversation. Feeling slightly awkward, I kept walking, fighting the urge to approach, to meet her right then and there.

At that moment, Aaron broke from the group and headed in my direction. Quickening his pace, he came up alongside me and gave me a friendly slap on the shoulder.

"Hey, dude, what's up?" he asked.

"Not much. You?"

"Oh, dude, went out this morning, and, man, were the waves gnarly. The Alaskan swell finally showed. I hit plenty of sixes and a few eight-footers. Man, it was awesome."

Aaron was a surfing demon. He lived, loved, and thought of nothing else. He preferred being on his board more than spending time at school or hanging out with his friends.

He'd say, "Surfing the ocean's tranquility transcends all of reality. Dude, it's not just a sport, it's a lifestyle."

We didn't socialize or run in the same clique at school but knew and respected each other from our times on the water.

We kept walking on into the parking lot.

"Catch ya later, dude," he said and veered off in another direction.

Before he could take two steps, I shouted, "Aaron, hold up. I gotta ask you a question."

He waited for me. "Yeah, whatcha need, man?"

"That girl you were speaking with back in the quad. Who is she?"

"Which one?"

"The blonde."

"Oh. . . . She's my neighbor, Opal. Why?"

"I don't know. . . . Okay, the truth is I've seen her before and think she's a babe."

"That's cool," he said. "You wanna meet her?"

"Sure, that would be—" he cut me off.

"Then follow me home and I'll introduce you. She lives a couple of houses down the street."

"You mean now?" I asked apprehensively.

"Dude, now! But let me warn you, man, don't mess with her head. I've known her a few years, and she's totally one of the nice ones."

"No way, Aaron. I just thought I wouldn't mind getting to know her. Get me the intro, and I'll take it from there."

"Cool. Let's book, then."

"Thanks," I replied, meaning it.

WITHOUT SKIPPING A beat, I high-stepped it over to my motorcycle, a Honda 125. It was a gift from my folks for my sixteenth birthday—best three hundred bucks they ever spent on me. I tailed his car like a dog sniffing the ground before marking his spot. I wasn't about to lose him due to an untimely red light or some errant jaywalker. The trip was short, a couple of miles at best, but then I began to wonder why he hadn't just introduced me at school. After all, she was standing right there.

Once I arrived at his house, I heaved the bike back onto its kickstand, turned the key off and sat. His house was enormous. All of the houses on the street were massive by my standards. Immediately, I felt out of place among the manicured lawns and multicolored exteriors. Part of me wanted to leave. I didn't belong in this part of town. But then I spotted Aaron sitting on his front porch, waving me over. It was too late now.

Leaving my backpack on the bike, I made my way up the red brick walkway.

"Aaron," I asked when I got to him, "why couldn't we do this at school?"

He gave me a knowing look, laughed to himself, and replied, "Hey, man, she was ready to catch her ride when I left . . . and her Mom's kinda strict. She likes her home right after school. So I figured you wouldn't mind some extra time with her. And, dude, what could be better than at her house . . . with her mom?" He chuckled. "You can thank me later," and then he laughed loudly.

Before I could answer, a brown station wagon passed to my left. Behind me and out of my field of vision, I heard the creak of a car door and then a girl, saying something like, "I'll see you tomorrow, Sandy," and "Thank you very much for the ride, Mrs. Zane."

Aaron quickly jumped over the porch's planter box and rushed toward her, shouting, "Hey, Opal, come here," while swinging his arm like an airplane propeller.

Absolutely unprepared, I stood, trying my best to smile. I was nervous, unusually so. Girls had always been easy for me. I was able to pick and choose, mostly playing upon their insecurities. I sensed this girl was different. I had a feeling my usual lines wouldn't play with her. Noticing my hands were shaking, I shoved them in my pockets and focused on Aaron, praying he wouldn't embarrass me.

She crossed the street without a word and stepped onto the lawn next to Aaron. There the three of us stood, no one saying anything. She looked at me; I looked at her, and then the both of us looked at Aaron. Aaron stared at me, then rolled his eyes as if to say, "Here you go, stud . . . take it from here." He glanced back at her and then they both started laughing, seemingly at some private joke.

"Okay, what's going on here?" I asked, actually thankful that the tension had been broken, but knowing something was amiss.

"Kent, this is Opal. Oh, you know, the kissing booth girl. And, Opal . . . Kent . . . the dude you thought was cute." He pointed to each of us in turn as he made the introductions.

"You guys have a lot in common, and it's time to find out about what." He abruptly stopped speaking, backed up, and walked away, chuckling, leaving us to our own devices. Wide-eyed, we watched him leave.

She spoke without hesitation.

"So, would you like to come over and talk for a while?"

After Aaron's gift for pleasantries, my heart was racing. With the most eloquent and literate vocabulary I could muster, I replied, "Sure."

Her house was across the street and two houses up on the right. It was two stories and a mirror image of Aaron's. We followed the brick front walk to the porch. To the right of the front door hung an old-fashioned wooden swing. Painted gray and suspended by four metal chains, it was one of those luxury items only the rich could afford and it fit in nicely with the place.

"Please sit. I'll be right back." She gave me what amounted to a halfhearted smile, though it came across as nervous. She opened the front door and went inside, leaving me alone.

Settle down, Kent, I thought. *So far, so good.*

In spite of my lack of communication skills, here I was, at her house, on her porch, sitting on her swing, waiting for her. Not bad for having said only one word to her.

Feeling calmer, I pushed the swing back, lifted my feet off the ground, and listened to the chains grind with each arc. In the background, I could hear her talking with someone, her mother, I assumed. The door opened, and she reappeared with a smug smile and sat down next to me, close, but not too close.

"You know, I saw you before," she said.

"When?" I asked, confident I knew the answer.

"A couple times my freshman year, and then, I think it was about a week before this last Sadie Hawkins Dance. You were in a group of five or six girls. I walked right by you."

"You sure? I would have remembered you," I responded flirtatiously, but not remembering in the least.

"Oh, I don't know about that. They seemed to have your undivided attention."

"I'm positive I didn't see you. The first time I saw you, you were in the kissing booth."

"Then why didn't you just come up? Were you afraid of little ol' me? I know how gorgeous I was with those penciled-in freckles and ponytails," she said, brushing her hair back off her shoulders.

"Actually, I tried, but the bell rang and then the next thing I knew, you were gone."

"I know," she said.

"What do you mean, you know?"

"I heard you were trying to find out who I was. What were they saying you called me? Oh yeah, Opal, the sophomore kissing booth girl?"

I felt my face burn with embarrassment. I couldn't believe she had actually called me out. People simply didn't blurt out things like that. Aaron's remark had been bad enough, but she had exposed me further, and I felt naked. Gathering what was left of my dignity, I asked, "Who told you that?"

She reached over and touched my forearm and said, "Relax, it's okay, I've wanted to meet you, too."

Ignoring her goodwill gesture, I pressed further.

"No, really, who told you?"

Retreating abruptly but still wearing a smile, she said, "A girl has her secrets, and this one I'm going to keep—for now."

"Yeah. . . . So it seems you might know more about me than I do about you." Conceding the battle, I changed the subject.

"It's my turn. Opal, tell me about yourself. I know you're a sophomore, live in this big house, and you're a friend of Aaron's. What else?"

"Well, yes, I'm a sophomore. I like school. Actually, I think it's easy. I have a best friend, Sandy. We've been friends for years and she's really nice, pretty too. What else? . . . I have three younger brothers: Timmy, Tony, and Oscar."

She began rubbing her hands together, and her ensuing speech became progressively faster and faster. She had just outed herself—she obviously felt awkward and uncomfortable talking about herself.

"My parents are from Ohio," she continued. "That's where I was born, too. Not my brothers, though. They were all born here. I like to camp, oh . . . our whole family likes to camp. You ever been to Oregon? The hills are beautiful there. Am I talking too much?"

"No, not at all. Actually, you're kinda cute when you blabber on." She started to turn red—first her cheeks, then her upper chest and neck.

"I do have a question," I said. "What's your last name? I have no idea what it is."

"Milton. I'm Opal Lynn Milton," she announced proudly, sitting straight up and then crossing her right leg over her left knee in an overtly feminine gesture.

"And who are you exactly, Miss Opal Lynn Milton? Those things you mentioned are all intriguing facts about yourself, but what I really want to know is, what lies underneath?"

She was silent for a minute and looked me straight in the eye, forcing me to look away. Her eyes were inviting, and before turning away, I noticed her pupils had enlarged. I read somewhere that when someone's pupils dilate it means they like the person they're looking at.

"Why?" she finally asked.

"I want to know the real Opal."

"I don't know," she said, again adjusting herself, this time crossing her right leg over and away from me.

I could tell she was giving it some thought. Was she going to be honest or feed me a line of bull? I stayed silent, giving her time to decide as I gazed upon her delicate lips.

She stared out into the street for a time and then finally replied, "I like waking up to rainy days and hearing the rain splash off the roof. Sometimes I curl up in bed and just listen. The sound of the water drops is magical. Dad says, for each raindrop that you hear, somebody's wish is being granted." She paused and then looked at me.

"I like the way I feel when I cry at a stupid romance movie. Oh . . . and I love the smell of Mom's homemade bread. One whiff two blocks away and I can tell she's been baking. . . . How's that?"

"Wow, that's good." *My god, who was this girl*, I thought. "I'm sure there's more, though. What else?"

"I can't tell you everything. We just met. Oh, I have a word for you."

"Yeah?"

"Patience."

Instantly, I knew I had met my match. She was smart, quick-witted, and wise well beyond her years. And she had no concept of how beautiful she was. We spent the next hour talking about many things. She had gone to the Sadie Hawkins dance with her girlfriend, Sandy, and knew I had turned down Meg at the last minute. She was trying out for the track team, went to church every Sunday, loved children, and wanted to be a teacher. We shared our ideas and beliefs, and surprisingly, found out we had much in common.

However, I deliberately listened more than I spoke, asked a lot of questions, and revealed very little. I wanted to believe she was safe, but I had never before let someone in. Maybe in time, but as she had earlier said to me, I would eventually say to her, "Patience."

When it was time to go, I didn't want to leave. As we said goodbye, there was no holding hands, no kiss goodbye, no meeting her parents, only an agreement to see each other again. We planned to meet at the library the following Tuesday night, right after dinner, to study together.

The promises of tomorrow . . .

Four

Whack . . .

Pain shot through my head as I fell to the floor. Barely conscious, I felt a trickle of blood down the back of my neck, then caught sight of the red fluid as it dripped onto the carpet. Regaining my senses, I lifted my head and used my hands to boost myself off the floor, all the while never taking my eyes off of him.

"Dad-gummit, don't you ever disrespect me again, boy. Next time I'll put you in the hospital!" the man bellowed.

Now on my feet, fists clenched, I towered over the smaller, thin man. He stood his ground, wielding a miniature baseball bat in his left hand—the kind they give away at Angels' bat night. With great effort, I focused and spoke in a composed and forceful voice.

"Listen, old man, I am going to tell you this just once, so take note, Daaaad. That will be the last time you will ever touch me." My jaw tightened with disdain. "Now that I'm facing you, let's see what kind of man you really are. I already know what kind you are when my back is turned. So, go ahead and swing. But if you do, I swear to God, I will kill you. That bat will be shoved so far down your throat it will take the coroner a week to remove it. Go ahead, try it again, you sorry excuse of a man."

My eyes were filled with a mocking rage, like a lion guarding its latest kill, daring any rivals to try and take it from him. I had grown two inches and put on thirty pounds over the past year, and I was brimming with a sense of power, feeling the effects of heightened adrenaline and testosterone coursing through my veins. I felt invincible, and finally, after years of beatings at this man's hands, I had decided today was the day it would end.

Surprised, the little man took a step back and lowered what he referred to as his "certainty stick."

"You're a lucky boy. I could have hit you a lot harder," he said, faltering slightly.

"Just shut up! I'm sick and tired of your mouth." I paused, letting my words sink in. "Don't you ever walk into our house again. You're not wanted here."

"You can't tell me what I can or can't do. I'm your—"

I took two steps toward him, ready to strike, but instead I shouted, "I don't give a shit who you are. You're dead to me. I never want to see or talk to you again. So get out, old man, before I seriously hurt you!"

Shoulders slumped, he spinelessly backed up to the door, feeling for the knob with his free hand. Getting in the last word, he murmured, "See, I made a man out of you," as he slithered out the door, slamming it behind him. I was rid of him—Wes, my so-called father.

Touching the back of my head I could feel a patch of crusted blood woven into the hair follicles and scalp. At its center was a wet, gaping gash about two inches long and still bleeding. I was thankful it wasn't a serious cut. Okay, that's not exactly true. I hoped it wasn't serious enough to require stitches.

I was glad that no one was home to witness the altercation; two fights in three weeks was a lot, even for me. Having just gotten off restriction, there was no way in hell I was going to tell Mom what had happened. Regardless of my explanation, I would have been the one to suffer the consequences. Mom had taught me well. Keeping secrets can keep you out of trouble, and the knowledge of them gives you power and control over others.

Nothing was going to interfere with my plans with Opal. I had two hours to clean the blood out of the green shag carpet and wash my T-shirt. That was easy. What would be harder was hiding the cut on the back of my head. She didn't need to know.

Secrets . . .

Five

The Tustin Library had recently moved from around the corner. It was substantially larger, with a vastly improved stock over its previous location. With most municipal buildings, bigger meant better, with the corollary of a slight loss of customer service. Furthermore, accompanying nearly all city expansions was the tendency to underestimate the new workload, resulting in an underpaid and overworked staff, adding to the already existing stigma that government workers are lazy.

Fortunately, Tustin was not one of those typical cities. Their library hired two additional employees to handle the increased workload, and as a result, had been able to maintain its warm, intimate atmosphere in the new building.

Before going in, I peered through the thick, brown-tinted glass doors to see if I could spot her. I had no luck and again found myself acutely anxious. My stomach ached. What was I so nervous about? She would be there. But what if she wasn't? Had she changed her mind? Maybe her parents wouldn't let her come. I wasn't even sure if she liked me. . . . What was the matter with me? What was I thinking? She was no different than any of the other girls.

Oh . . . that's good, now I was lying to myself. After only a few hours with her, I already knew she was special. I opened the doors, walked through the foyer, and there in front of the reception area, I had my answer.

She was sitting at a table in the heart of the open expanse of the library, away from any window, but in an area where she couldn't be missed. She had her books strewn across the table. Pretending she had not seen me come in, she glanced up, and I felt her eyes touch me. She leaned back slightly, smiled, and exhaled powerfully, as if she too were relieved. I approached with my backpack in tow and returned her smile.

Leaning over, I whispered into her ear, "Hey, Disney girl, glad you're here," and sat down. The faint scent of her strawberry conditioner lingered in my nostrils.

"Of course, where else would I be?" She responded confidently. "What's with the Disney girl crack?"

"I just heard a song on the radio a few minutes ago that reminded me of you. It was called 'Disney Girls.'"

"Meaning?"

"No meaning. It was a happy song. It's a guy singing about good times with a girl of his. Not that you're my girl . . . it just reminded me of you."

What am I rambling on about?

I felt her eyes piercing my words and looking directly into my soul. I chose to look past her and sat down, avoiding eye contact.

"So, what you're saying is you've been thinking about me. Hmmm . . . ," she countered.

"No—yes—no . . . ," I replied, realizing she had trapped me with my own words.

"Tell me, do you think about me every second or only a few times a day?" she asked, giggling.

Conscious that she had let me off the hook, I tried a different tack.

"Miss Milton, I will have you know that I don't think about you every second or even a few times a day. I think about you every other second, but never when I'm driving. Otherwise I could end up in a ditch or wrapped around a telephone pole. Thus, whatever assumptions you may have made about me, they are completely and utterly wrong."

"Shhhhh . . . ," came a voice, clearly directed at me. It was the librarian.

Opal giggled even louder and quickly clapped her hands over her mouth. But instead of a muffled laugh, the sound expelled from behind her hands mimicked a fart in form and depth of vibration, not to mention it could be heard throughout the library.

Struggling to stifle my own laughter, I made matters worse by leaning too far back in my chair and falling onto the floor. Sprawled out, looking up, I saw Opal's face, tears now streaming down her cheeks. She couldn't stop laughing, try as she might.

Sensing all eyes on us, in a cracked voice I said, "We need to get out of here."

"What about your homework?" she asked, trying to stop her own voice from going another octave higher.

"Done. Did it before I came."

"Me too."

Leaving our books behind, we made a quick getaway, seconds before Opal added a quick snort to her already ornate symphony of laughter. Once outside, I gave in to full-fledged hysteria.

AROUND THE CORNER we ran, her holding onto my forearm as I pulled her along. I slowed to a walk, but she didn't anticipate my sudden deceleration and ran into my back giving me a surprise hug. As she quickly released me, our laughter evaporated, almost as if this contact was too much, too soon.

We headed toward the Old Town part of Tustin. The boulevard was well-lit with old-fashioned streetlights throwing eerie shadows onto the brick buildings from the ancient ficus trees. We walked for a few minutes without speaking, occasionally glancing at each other. The night was slightly chilly. I kept my hands in my pockets to keep them warm. In between the laughter at the library and the current silence, I wondered how it would feel to hold her hand—to feel her small, soft hand touching mine, to have our fingers intertwined. Something so simple, so innocent, struck such fear in my heart. While I was lost in thought, she bumped me, almost sending me off the sidewalk and into the street.

"What was that for?" I asked, righting myself.

"Well, you were so quiet. Tell me, what were you thinking about?"

"I think I talk too much around you."

"Kent, not even," she said. "Actually, I really know very little about you. I know you're funny and maybe a little cute, not much else."

I remained silent. I wanted to hold her hand.

"Okay, let's start with something easy. I've never seen you wear a ball cap before. You an Angel fan?"

She grabbed the cap off my head and was about to place it on her own, and then stopped.

"Why is it wet?" she asked, feeling inside the cap. She moved the cap into the light, and looked more closely. "This is blood. Are you bleeding?"

"Oh, it's nothing," I said. I reached my hand to the back of my head and felt where the hair had become soggy. The Band-Aid must have fallen off and the wound reopened.

"Let me see, then," she said.

"No, really, I'm fine."

"Come over here in the light. I want to see."

Grabbing me by the hand, she led me to the corner streetlight where she had enough light to see the cut clearly. I didn't want her to ask any more questions. I felt myself closing up.

"Bend over," she ordered. "Ouch. . . . You need to see a doctor."

"Really, it's okay. Another Band-Aid and I'll be fine."

She moved around to face me.

"What happened? And I want the truth."

"Why? What do you care?"

Once again grabbing my hand, she said, "Listen, I'm really trying here. You need to let me in. If you want this relationship to work, there are things I need to know . . . and this is one of them."

"You want a relationship?"

"Of course, you silly boy. Why else would I be here?"

"But you said you knew so little about me and . . ."

"Absolutely, I don't know a lot about you. I don't know your favorite color, how many brothers or sisters you have, or even exactly where you live. But, what I do know is more important than what kind of food you like or what your favorite sport is. I like the type of guy you are. I know underneath that tough, quiet guy exterior of yours, you're really a teddy bear. I know you're sweet, kind, and would never lie to me. So you can tell me, what happened?"

She had nailed me on every point. There was no resisting her honest heart. I broke down and told her every sordid detail of the day's events, starting with how I found Dad in the house going through our mail, asking him what he was doing there when no one was home, and being cracked over the head with the stick in response. I told her the story of the certainty stick and what I said to him that made him leave. But that's where I stopped. I didn't go into our history or how I felt about him. I was thankful she hadn't asked because I wouldn't have answered.

She was right, though. I had to make a decision, either open up and reveal what was below the surface or never see her again. I was well-versed in deflecting personal issues. I chose to avoid, run, or end relationships rather than expose myself to the scrutiny of another person. I found it easier to fight than to reveal my loneliness or the heartbreak of my family. But with Opal it was somehow okay. I wanted to believe in her, to trust her. Could she be the one?

We walked back to the library hand in hand. A huge smile was plastered all over my face. Once inside, she borrowed the library's first aid kit and cleaned my cut and placed a new Band-Aid on it. Then it was time for her to leave. Her mother picked her up and she waved goodbye as they drove off. I wondered. Maybe . . .

To trust is to give a gift of the heart.

Six

Over the next few weeks we talked endlessly, either by phone or on walks when we were supposed to be studying at the library. Gradually, I started to feel at ease with her. I began to believe I could tell her anything, but still held back when it came to some things that were just too painful to talk about. Trust was an especially difficult concept and one I wasn't too familiar with.

Grandpa Heil was the only person in whom I had any semblance of trust. When I was younger, Mom encouraged, no, guilted me into spending summers with her stepfather and mother.

She would say, "Grandpa works real hard. You could learn a lesson or two from him."

Of course I knew her real reason; she just wanted me out of the house. It was a break for her. Regardless of her intent, I always enjoyed our time together.

My Grandpa Heil was a real man. He had large hands, heavily callused from a lifetime of working with them. He owned a muffler shop, and my image of him was of him welding car piping with a cigarette hanging from his mouth. He often spoke in jaded, crude terms. Men feared his temper, yet they wanted to be around him. Beneath his hard exterior and coarse disposition, he had a gentle soul.

I spent many of my pre-teen summer days working for him. I would clean, sweep, and hand down tools to him in the muffler pit area. "The bowl," as he called it, was an open air basement structure dug six feet in the ground with walls of gray cinderblock. From inside the bowl, he could work on a car's undercarriage, suspended on two long steel ramps. A large metal hydraulic pole held the ramp assembly together and could be lowered or raised.

On rare occasions, a choice cuss word would escape his mouth.

"Don't tell your grandmother," he'd say. "She'd skin me alive."

His statement wasn't so much an order but confirmation of our unspoken bond. I rolled him countless cigarettes with the aid of his favorite red roller, and by the end of each stay, the smokes I manufactured were as good as any brand-name cigarettes, both in quality and firmness of pack.

He'd say, "Good smoke, son," and rub my head.

That was his way of saying "I love you."

Unfortunately, since Mom's latest marriage, getting to San Diego had become a problem. For some reason, Mom stopped making the two-hour trip. It was as if they had had some kind of falling out. Apart from holidays, I didn't see much of Grandpa anymore, but I always knew he was proud of me and loved me unconditionally. I had told Opal about him, and she understood his place in my life. Someday I hoped they would meet.

* * * * *

OPAL INVITED ME to dinner that Saturday night. She wanted me to arrive early so we could spend as much time together as possible. I didn't waver and accepted on the spot. I genuinely looked forward to meeting her parents. I was confident I could put on a good front.

FOUR O'CLOCK SHARP on Saturday afternoon, I rode up on my motorcycle. Dressed in my best Levis, the only pair free of holes, an Ocean Pacific shirt, and a light jacket, I felt presentable. I was usually a success with a girl's parents, as long as I treated them with respect and used good manners. A "Yes, sir" this and a "No, ma'am" that, and they were satisfied that I was an honest, upright young man. Though if they really knew what my intentions were, they wouldn't have been so quick to let their daughters out of the house. But today, with Opal, it was different. It was for the proverbial "all the marbles." The first impression really counted. It was like practicing catch for the big game. Only now it was showtime—the stadium was full and everything depended on my catching the Hail Mary pass with no time left. If I caught it, I'd be the star. If not, I'd go home a loser, alone, possibly never to return.

I knocked once, and the door opened immediately.

"Well, it's about time," Opal said impatiently. She smiled, grabbed my hand, and led me through the front hall, past the staircase and straight into the family room.

The room was large and elaborately decorated with all the accoutrements of a family with money. Highly polished tables, overstuffed chairs, and several framed paintings filled the space with ease. The oversized red brick fireplace was the room's focal point, a collection of family photos adorning its mantel. To the left of it, in the corner, the television was playing a familiar cartoon. Instantly I recognized "The Flintstones" from my many years of being babysat by the TV. On the other side was a set of sliding glass doors, with the curtains pulled back, a pool and Jacuzzi beyond.

On the floor, two little boys were playing with Lego blocks. Opal's father sat next to them in an armchair and stood up to greet me as I entered.

"Nice to meet you, son. And your name is?" he asked as he extended his hand.

"I'm Kent," I replied, shaking his hand.

"Oh stop it, Dad, you know who he is," Opal chided.

"Over there are my boys, Timmy and Tony," Mr. Milton said, with a chuckle. The boys looked up, gave a wave, and without pause, went back to playing.

"Where's Mom?" Opal asked.

"She's waking little Oscar. She should be down in a minute," he replied.

"Have a seat, son, and tell me about your plans for the future. Do they include my daughter?" he asked.

"Dad! Stop it, that's enough. I'm taking him into the other room and away from you," she sounded irritated.

She touched my arm and then tugged, not so subtly urging me to come with her. We left her father standing there, palms up, saying innocently, "What? What did I do now?" wearing a devilish grin.

She led me back to the front of the house and into the formal living room. Sitting on the fancy embroidered couch, I kept repositioning myself, trying to get comfortable among the many throw pillows. I took two off and handed them to her, unsure what else to do with them.

"Sorry about my dad," she said while placing the pillows on a chair next to her. "You're the first guy I've ever had over, and he's acting all weird. He's trying to embarrass me."

"That's okay. I'm fine talking to him. Actually, I have a few questions for him," I replied.

"About?"

"About you."

"Oh, no, you don't. We're staying right here," she insisted.

"Hello?" came a voice from just outside the room. I stood, anticipating her mother's entrance.

"Hi, I'm Kent," I said as she came in. She was not at all what I had been expecting, several inches taller than Opal and looking nothing like her. Her hair was a mousy brown color, and freckles covered every inch of visible skin, face, arms, and legs. Clearly Opal got her looks from her dad's side of the family.

"Pleasure to meet you. Please call me Mrs. Milton. Sit," she said while taking a seat herself on the matching chair directly in front of me.

"Mom, come on, I just went through this with Dad," Opal begged. "Besides, you'll have plenty of time to talk to him at the dinner table."

"It's all right, Opal," I said reassuringly. "She just got here."

"Wonderful. Now, Opal speaks very highly of you. Please tell me about yourself."

"Well, ma'am, there's not really a whole lot to say. Let's see, I'm a junior at Tustin. I play football, I'm on the debate team, like to surf. Uuuh, I have an older sister who's a senior at Tustin, too."

"My, that's nice. Do you have any other siblings?"

"Yes. I have a younger brother, Danny. He's in eighth grade."

"And your parents," Mrs. Milton continued, "how long have they been married?"

I hesitated, suddenly realizing I'd waded into treacherous waters, but I wouldn't lie. I wanted her to like me.

"Mom and my stepfather have been married for three, maybe four years."

"Then this is your mother's second marriage." She paused and then asked, "Are you able to see much of your father?"

"Actually, no, ma'am," I corrected her. "This is Mom's third marriage. And I really don't see my dad too much," I said, relieved that my head wound had healed quickly. Then I wondered what exactly Opal had told her mom about me. Had she broken our bond and revealed my secret about the fight with Dad?

When I glanced at Opal, she had a look of surprise on her face and not a good one either.

"Mom, this is way too serious. Can you lighten it up, please?"

"Sure thing, honey. I'll tell you what, I'll get started on dinner and leave you two be."

"Thanks, Mom."

Mrs. Milton left the room, and Opal immediately gave me a stare that could have killed a dead man. In a low whisper she said, "We need to go for a walk."

I had liked walks up until then.

Seven

Once out the door, she was a good two paces ahead of me. I finally caught up when we got to the corner of her street. I grabbed her hand and she abruptly yanked it away.

"What's the matter?" I asked.

"I can't believe you. I brought you into my home, had you meet my family, and most of all, let you into my heart, and this is how you treat me," she cried.

"Why? What have I done?"

"Listen, I explained before that you had to let me in if you wanted a relationship, which implied we talk about everything, the good, the bad, and whatever's in between. Meaning we have no secrets. I promise you there isn't anything you could tell me that I couldn't handle—we can't handle—together. We have to be a team. I don't like being surprised in front of my family like that. Why didn't you tell me your mom was on her third marriage? The number of times she's been married isn't important, it's that you didn't tell me first."

"Yeah. But before I answer, first tell me what you told your parents about me. Did you say I was some poor guy you're taking pity on, who had a putrid excuse for a dad that beat the crap out of his kids?"

"Kent, what are you talking about? I wouldn't do that. I would never tell anyone what we talk about. It's our relationship and only about us. Obviously you haven't quite figured that one out yet."

"Okay, so what did you tell her?" I asked again.

"I said you were nice and kind-hearted. I asked them not to judge you because you look different with that long hair of yours and drive a motorcycle. I told them you are really special and treat me like a princess. Mostly, though, I said I liked you because you were different."

"Oh . . . ," I paused. "There you go again. How is it every time you can make me feel so damned stupid?"

"Because that's who I am. So, what's it gonna be, Surfer Boy? Do you want me or not? Cause if you're going to break my heart, you better do it right now."

"All right, sure, I get your point." I paused. "The truth is I've been thinking about, you know . . . about this whole opening up thing." Searching for the right words, I went on, "But you have to understand, it's hard for me. I've never let anyone in before, and you're asking for everything. I'm not used to that. Have a little faith and patience, because I really do want us to work out."

"Finally. It's about time I got some real emotion out of you," she said.

"You want emotion?" I pulled her close and hugged her solidly. The feel of her body as she returned the embrace reinforced my conviction that I had made the right decision. I would allow myself to be cared for . . . and maybe even loved.

I spoke quietly into her ear, "I could never break your heart."

She squeezed tighter.

IN THE NEW belief that there was an us, we walked a good mile over the next fifteen minutes. For the first time, it felt like a bona fide relationship. We had argued and nobody left. That in itself was a new experience for me. She was a year younger than I was, yet so much wiser and more mature in her understanding of what it took to have a relationship. My mom could have learned a few things from her.

With my hand in hers, aimlessly wandering the streets, I smiled, feeling lucky to have this girl in my life. As we got closer to her house, the smile I had worn so proudly during our walk gradually dissipated. Making a good impression for Opal's sake now took on even greater importance. Stopping on the top step to the front porch, I pulled her back.

"Listen, I know your parents may ask some questions, personal stuff about me, and you might not know the answer. It's not a reflection on you or on us. I want to be honest with them for you. They need to get to know me. If there's something you don't understand or we haven't talked about before, just go with it. We can always talk about it later. Okay?"

"It will be fine; we're fine. I know where your heart is." She placed her hands on my chest, raised herself up on her tiptoes and gave me a quick kiss on the cheek.

If I wasn't content before, I was on top of the world at that moment. I felt myself evolving. As to what exactly was changing, I wasn't sure, but I knew something good was happening. I wondered if this was what it felt like to be happy.

BACK INSIDE, HER parents were gentle and unusually considerate of me. They were much less inquisitive and it seemed as if they'd had a discussion of their own about how to treat Opal's new friend. Whatever the reason, I welcomed the difference.

At dinner, Mr. Milton said grace while they all bowed their heads. I went along, wanting to respect the house rules. Everyone was on their best behavior, including her three younger brothers, in spite of their complaints about "eating in the big room" instead of at the regular dinner table. I felt honored that Opal had made it special for me, particularly when eating in the formal dining room was reserved for special occasions and holidays.

Afterward, Opal cleared the table while her mother ushered the boys into the next room, leaving Mr. Milton alone with me.

"Son, I see you have a motorcycle out there," he said.

"Yes, sir," I answered respectfully. "It's a Honda 125. It's small, but it gets me around."

"That's great, son. But there are a couple of things I want to get straight with you. First, you will not take my daughter out on it. Do you understand?"

"Yes, sir."

Oh, man, is he trying to intimidate me or what? I thought.

"Second, where's your helmet? Do you know how many people die or get maimed each year riding without one? Please wear one, if not for yourself, then for our benefit."

I felt like a small child being chastised for not looking both ways before crossing the street.

"Yes, sir," I answered dutifully. "I do have one that I can wear." Believing in my words, I bent to the possibility of actually wearing one—at least to and from their house. In truth, I preferred the air in my face, much like a dog enjoys sticking his head out of a car window. But for her, I could change.

"Good. With that being said, son, I'd like to welcome you into our home anytime."

What did he just say? He'd said I was welcome here. I couldn't have predicted that one. "Thank you," I responded, beaming.

Just then, Opal walked into the room.

"Okay, Dad, what are guys talking about?" she asked.

"What, honey?" he replied, placing his hands flat on the table with a gentle thump.

"Why is he smiling and why did you guys quit talking as soon as I walked in?"

Turning her attention to me, she asked, "What did he say? Did he tell you something funny about me?"

"Honestly, we weren't talking about you. Aren't you being a little paranoid?" I joked.

"Shush, you would be too if you knew my dad," she said, redirecting her attention to her father, glaring, eyes narrowed.

In a serious tone, Mr. Milton responded, "Honey, we were just talking. Nothing to do with you. It's fine."

"Sure, Dad. But if I find out otherwise, I'll . . . I'll . . . I'll tell Mom."

Unfamiliar with the family's dynamic, I assumed telling Mom would be a bad thing. Mr. Milton and I just looked at each other and started laughing.

THE REST OF the night was filled with good questions, exchanges of views on general issues, nothing too complex or personal. When it came time to leave, I gave her parents the usual platitudes: "You have a beautiful home," "Dinner was great," and finally, "Thank you for your hospitality."

Feeling that the day couldn't have gone any better, I was proved wrong again as Opal walked me out. I was about to throw my leg over the bike when she grabbed a fistful of my jacket.

"Wait, didn't you forget something?" she asked, appearing frustrated.

Looking around, I checked my hands and then felt my jackets pockets.

"No, don't think so."

"How about me?"

What was I thinking? This was the moment I had longed for. As with every incident this night, this too was unexpected. Ardently I stepped forward, bent slightly and slowly leaned in. Feeling her breath on my lips was a sensation unequal to anything I had ever experienced. We kissed, gently at first, with closed mouths, then simultaneously our lips parted and breaths exchanged. Her taste was sweet, with a hint of cherries. We unhurriedly withdrew and closed our mouths, yet not far enough—a single saliva string still connected us.

She moved her head to my shoulder and hugged me tightly. She said, "You were great with my parents. Thank you."

"You're very lucky to have such a family. No wonder I think you're extraordinary."

Pulling back and looking her straight in the eye, I said, "Guess what your dad said to me."

"What?"

"He said I'm welcome here anytime."

"No. Really?" she said, surprised. She smiled and clutched me again, moving her hand to the back of my head.

"Yes, really. Truthfully, this has been one of the best days of my life. Thanks for inviting me."

I stood straight up, shifting so her hands could no longer reach the back of my head. I knew the wound had healed, but it had left a different kind of scar.

With another quick kiss goodbye, a peck this time, I pressed the ignition, gave it a little gas, waved, and drove off. With the wind flowing through my hair, I felt free to be me.

Seeds of change begin with roots; some are buried deeper than others.

Eight

As time passed, we fell into a regular routine. Mondays through Thursdays we'd meet at the library, usually after dinner. If we couldn't meet, we'd talk incessantly on the phone. Weekends, I was allowed to see her on Friday or Saturday night, never both, nor on Sundays.

In the meantime, the Homecoming dance, Thanksgiving and Christmas came and went. She gave me a bottle of cologne, English Leather, and I gave her two albums, Crosby, Stills, Nash & Young's "So Far" and an Emerson, Lake & Palmer record my sister recommended. She smiled as if she liked them. Regardless of the gifts, we were just happy being together.

Because of our ages, we had conditions placed on us, or rather she did. The amount of time she could spend with me was strictly limited by her parents, and rarely were we ever alone, except for our walks. However, as it is with most teenagers, there is always a way, and we found ours.

THE FRIDAY BEFORE school started back following Christmas break, we had that opportunity. Opal got permission to go to a bonfire in Huntington Beach. I may have stretched the truth a bit when I said that others would be there. In fact, there would be other people around—we just didn't know them— nor were they invited to our particular get-together.

I picked her up around four thirty in the afternoon. I had asked her to dress warmly because nights can get cold on the beach. Having withdrawn a big chunk of my savings for that night's date, I meticulously planned everything from flowers to food, including borrowing Mom's new '74 Monte Carlo— at least new to us. Earlier, I had packed the car's trunk full of the essentials for our romantic interlude.

Forever the gentleman, I opened the car door for her and then backed away, paying attention to her expression. A single red rose rested on the seat. She gasped and gave a short, timid laugh as she covered her mouth with her hand. Picking up the flower and holding it to her nose, she asked "Is this for me?"

"Of course," I replied.

Closing the door and walking around the front of the car, I watched her nuzzle the petals, inhaling their perfume, although her eyes remained squarely on me as I rounded the vehicle and climbed into my seat.

"Thank you," she said, and leaned over to kiss my cheek.

Turning to her, I declared, "Tonight, it's all about us. I have so much to share with you."

"Like what?"

"You'll see."

"Oh, come on. Give me a hint," she pleaded.

"Like I said, it's all about us."

She poked me in the side once, then twice. It tickled—and I mean a lot—my greatest weakness had been exposed. I'm extremely ticklish, and now that she'd found my spot, she didn't let up.

"Okay, okay, I'll tell you."

She stopped and placed her hands in her lap.

"Tonight," I said, "you can ask me anything and I won't dodge it. No more talking around issues anymore, it's just about you and me, honestly."

Looking away, I started the ignition and drove without saying anything more. I could tell she was thinking. I assumed she was calculating her next line of questioning. I wondered just how far she was going to take it. But it didn't matter—nothing was out of bounds.

Instead, she grabbed my hand, gave it a squeeze, and paralyzed me by saying, "I already know what I need to know."

I finally understood. I got it. It was never about opening up and exposing every intimate detail of my life but about my willingness and desire to share with her. That's what she had always wanted from me. I clasped her hand firmly, wanting never to let go. I was in love.

Either by fate or coincidence, she turned on the radio and the song "Disney Girls" played. She said softly, "I love it," and sang along, seeming to know the lyrics.

"You know the words?" I asked.

"Of course I do, silly. It's your song about me. Did you know it wasn't originally sung by Art Garfunkel?"

"Huh. . . . What?"

"Yeah, kinda surprised me, too. The Beach Boys recorded it in 1971, as did Mama Cass Elliot. I believe Bruce Johnston wrote it back in 1957. Did you know he was a Beach Boy? Really, more of an on-again-off-again Beach Boy. So Art Garfunkel wasn't the first to record it. Still, pretty cool, though. It was written way before we were born."

"How do you know this stuff?"

"Believe it or not, I'm pretty smart, not just a dumb blonde. And certainly not like any other girl you've dated before." She laughed assertively while avoiding my solemn, humorless glare.

"And what exactly have you heard?" I asked.

"Nothing, I just know some of the girls you've dated, and I wouldn't consider any of them intelligent. That's all."

Ouch, that hurts. I knew she was only kidding, but it still stung. There was no doubt she was right, but she was even sharper than I had expected. My dating history was a no-brainer, and I needed to get her off that topic. Switching gears, I asked, "Back to the song for a sec, how'd you know its history?"

"Well, I bought the album after you first told me about it. Then I researched the song at the library. In fact, it was funny how I did my investigation right in front of you. And . . . you never knew," she snickered.

"You're awful proud of yourself, aren't you?"

"Why, yes, I am. I don't usually have much on you. So anytime I can get one up, I'll take it. You know, it's only because I lo—" She stopped mid-sentence and gave my hand another squeeze.

"So, what was that? What were you going to say?" I nudged her, hoping she would get the hint that I wanted more. If it was what I thought, I needed to hear it.

Instead, she became very quiet. Silence filled the car. Hand-stroking took over as our alternative form of communication. She rested her head on my shoulder, yet not another word was uttered until we arrived at the beach's main entrance.

* * * * * *

HUNTINGTON STATE BEACH is a state park that covers about two miles of pristine Southern Californian coastline. It's used for bicycling, surf fishing, skating, and people watching. But its main draw is the surfing. People from all over the world come to surf the waves. Because of the natural curve of the coastline, it faces southwest and often receives strong surf called "south swells." These large swells are born in storms originating either in the South Pacific off New Zealand or the Mexican coast, or a combination of both.

After paying the entry fee, we drove south toward my destination, as I silently prayed it would be unoccupied. Familiar with the Surf City's beach layout, I had selected the last set of fire rings, knowing they were usually secluded and private. It was the perfect romantic spot, a good distance from the main entrance and in an area where most tourists didn't venture unless they happened to stumble onto it.

Swinging the car around, I backed into one of the many available parking spaces. Our car was one of only two vehicles in an otherwise empty lot. The other car, an older, green VW Bug, was parked at the opposite end. Bathrooms bookended the parking lot. They were visible from a good distance with their freshly painted white walls and teal-colored frame accents.

I popped the trunk using the interior power trunk release and quickly got out to open her door.

Positioning myself between Opal and the trunk, I discreetly pulled out a heavy sweater, thicker than what she had on. I convinced her to put it on as she wouldn't be warm enough otherwise, all the while being careful to obscure her view of the trunk's contents. I pointed her to the restroom where she could change.

Before letting her walk off, from behind my back I pulled out a second red rose and presented it to her. She was uncharacteristically quiet. She took the rose with a forced smile, and I began to wonder if something was wrong.

Once she left, I brushed aside my unease and immediately got to work. Opening the trunk wide, I loaded my arms with several bundles of firewood. After two quick trips, the fire ring was stocked with enough wood for a good-sized blaze. I stacked the leftover timber outside the concrete ring and hurried back to the car to gather the rest of the supplies. Two blankets, lighter fluid, a radio, a box of matches, and two champagne glasses. On my final trip I pulled out the ice chest, beach chairs, and two more roses.

Just as I returned to the car to close the trunk, she came out of the restroom. The blue and white sweater she now wore was obviously oversized on her small frame, but she looked comfortable, having rolled up the sleeves multiple times. I had expected her to take her time changing, and I was right. She had always been concerned about her appearance, not in a vain way, but rather out of a desire to be presentable at all times, in the most modest sense. I was sure she had spent extra time ensuring that the sweater looked respectable, and then there was the hair. She was very particular about her hair, and the end result was always worth the effort.

Meeting her where the sand encroached on the asphalt, I offered up the third red rose. She took it instantly, adding it to the others, and hugged me.

"You don't have any more back there, do you?" she asked. She groped around behind my back, searching for more.

"Follow me, sweetheart," I said.

Stepping onto the sand, she suddenly stopped, sat down, and took off her shoes while I stood waiting impatiently.

"I'm ready," she said, picking up her roses in one hand and handing me her shoes with the other so that we could hold hands. "Lead on."

Thirty yards later and feeling the sand in my shoes, I watched her eyes light up as we approached the fire ring. There hadn't been enough time to start the fire, but there was sufficient light from the setting sun for her to appreciate my handiwork. Everything was in its place. I had spread out the larger of the blankets next to the fire ring; two beach chairs were set out, one holding a radio on its seat. On the concrete ledge of the fire ring, a single white rose lay between the two champagne glasses.

Noticing the rose, she let go of my hand and jumped onto the blanket, bringing sand along with her. She added the three previous flowers to the white rose on the ledge.

"Are you going to light it or what?" she requested.

Her behavior was a little strange, even for her. Something was up, and I couldn't quite put my finger on it.

"When you're done with the fire, you wanna fight?" She kneeled, fists clenched, moving them in a circle in a parody of a boxer.

Completely puzzled by this new personality, I focused on starting the fire. I squirted a generous portion of lighter fluid onto the logs, arranged in a pyramid, from the largest to the smallest for the maximum burn potential. I tossed in a lit match, which set off a mini-explosion, but the fire soon settled into a nice, even flame.

Returning my attention to her, I said, "Listen, Opal, if we're going to fight, at least place your thumbs on the outside of your fingers. Otherwise you could break a thumb."

"How's this?" She showed me her corrected fists.

"Perfect." Picking up the ice chest, I placed it next to the blanket for easy access. Flipping the lid open I started pulling out one item at a time. First, a small glass vase, which I handed to her so she could place the roses in it. Next, a full plate of cheeses and crackers held in place with cellophane wrap. Finally, buried amongst the ice cubes, I pulled out a chilled bottle of Brut Champagne. Sissy had gotten one of her friends to buy it for me. All I had to do was fork over the bucks.

"Well, you have thought of everything, haven't you?" she asked.

Looking deeply into her eyes, I said, "I wanted tonight to be very special. I had to show you because, you know, my words don't always express how I really feel."

She inched toward me. In the firelight, her eyes glistened and I noticed a tear form and then spill down her left cheek.

"What's wrong?" I asked, beyond baffled.

She leaned forward, paused, and before our lips touched, she whispered, "I love you."

The fire crackled . . .

Nine

Throughout my life, I have experienced a handful of moments that I call a "soul's high." Difficult to describe, it's like a euphoric flash of the past and present blended, lasting anywhere from a few seconds to several minutes, and the memory of one can last a lifetime. It's a feeling that all is right with the world; when your heart, mind, and soul are pure and in alignment; a transcendent state of mind where you feel as if anything is possible. It's the sensation of complete satisfaction; where there is no negativity, no pain, no heartache or loneliness, no fear of what tomorrow might bring, nor want of anything outside of the present moment. An indescribable calm surrounds and envelopes you and all of life seems somehow connected in a unique, harmonious rhythm. You are content, fulfilled . . . happy.

Of course, not everyone has experienced a soul's high. It's like a marathon runner trying to explain a runner's high. Words help, but unless you have actually experienced it, it is very difficult to convey that exact feeling.

That night, when Opal first said, "I love you," was my first soul's high. In that moment, I saw the world in another way. I could believe in concepts like honesty and trust. I was different. I had a new hope . . . for me.

We lay on the blanket and kissed passionately. Pulling away from her lips, breathing slowly but heavily, I mouthed the words, "I love you," barely audible above the crackle and sputter of the fire. She held me tighter.

As I released her and gazed into her eyes, I could see they were welling up again. New tears gathered, and with the momentum of their own weight, rolled down her cheeks. She buried her face in my chest as if to hide them from me.

"Don't, Opal. It's okay," I said. Touching her face, I wiped away the droplets. "I hope you're crying tears of joy. Hey, there's no need to turn away. There's no shame between us."

"I know." More tears streamed down. "Can you ever love someone too much? Because that's how I feel about you," she said.

I didn't reply. I didn't know. So instead, I held her for several minutes, taking in love's aura. She listened to my heartbeat, and she said it was deafening compared to the roar of the fire or crash of the distant waves.

To lighten the mood, I teasingly asked, "You know why you cry, don't you?"

"Yeah, it's when you're really happy or sad," she said softly, but in a tone suggesting that I was an idiot.

"Well, let me tell you a little story about what really happens when you cry." Sitting up, I continued, "Now, picture this: think of your brain as its own little environment. When you're happy you have clear skies, flowers bloom, all of your senses are on high. You see colors more clearly, you can smell things better, and the touch. . . . Ah, the touch . . . it's just good. Here, feel."

I extended my arm to her and she touched it lightly and then with a caress.

"Ooooh. That's niiiiiiiice," I joked.

"Stop it."

She jerked her hand back as if my arm were a hot plate straight out of the oven.

I went on, "But when you're sad, clouds start to form. And if you're sad enough, the clouds begin to rain. Yes, it actually rains on your brain, and then the rain water drains down into your eye sockets. Eventually, the water seeps out of your eyes. You know them as tears."

"You dork," she said. "Nice story."

"Oh wait, it gets better. When it thunders, you know, it's that noise you make when you cry real hard, yep, that's thunder. Then it's just a matter of time before it pours bucket loads of rain on your brain, and since your eyes are already filled to capacity, it causes the nose to react. Sure, your nose tries building dams up there. You can tell when you get all stuffed up. But if your nose starts to run, you know the dam's burst."

Shaking her head, she giggled. "Nah . . . you silly boy."

"Maybe not . . . but you stopped crying. And made you laugh, too, now didn't I?"

Slapping my arm, she said, "Not fair."

I grabbed her and pressed my weight against hers, gently easing her down from her seated position to where I lay directly on top of her, facing her, blue eyes to blue eyes.

"Opal, you mean so much to me. I love you." I wanted to say more, something romantic or charming, but I didn't have the words.

Her eyes still red, she spoke, "Oh . . . you have no idea how much I love you. I think about you every second. When I'm not with you, I want to be with you. Even when I'm with you, I somehow want more of you."

Unaccustomed to such raw emotion, I found myself unable to put two comprehensible syllables together. In place of words, I leaned down and kissed her.

We spent the next few hours kissing, holding each other, and talking of our love, next to the burning embers of the fire.

Sadly, the night had to end.

"Sweetheart, it's time to go."

I said the words, wishing they weren't true.

"The one thing I don't want to do is alienate your folks by bringing you home late," I said, wanting only to kiss her.

As I helped her up, she said, "Before we go, I have something for you." She jumped up, ran to the car, retrieved her purse and ran back. Sitting back down on the blanket, out of breath, she reached into the purse, pulled out an envelope and handed it to me.

I opened the unsealed envelope, removed a card and began reading. Finding it difficult to make out the words on the front by the dim firelight, I opened it up, hoping the inside might be easier to read. My eyes were drawn to the bottom where she had written in her own distinctive, left-leaning, cursive lettering, "I have found love in you. Forever . . . Opal."

My heart sank, not out of disappointment or sadness, but with the weight of having it filled up with so much love.

"Thank you. This is great. I love it," I said, looking into her eyes.

"I was going to give it to you earlier but kinda chickened out," she said, looking away.

"Okaaay . . . now I get it."

"What?" she asked.

"That's why you were acting so strange."

"What?" she repeated.

"In the car, you stopped yourself in mid-sentence. You were going to say it right then, right?"

"Maybe."

"What was that about? Before, you couldn't stop talking. All right—I'm used to that part, but this time you talked a lot about nothing. Then you got all weird and didn't say anything the rest of the trip. After that you wanted to fight me."

"Well, I was nervous. I wasn't sure how you would react."

"Really? You weren't sure how I'd react?"

"I know . . . I was stupid. Besides, you're the first person I've ever said it to—who wasn't family. And you didn't help much either."

"I didn't help? How about the roses, the music, or the roaring fire?"

"No, all that was perfect, and you made tonight very special. Oh . . . I don't know. It was just scary for me."

"I understand. But, from now on, if you ever feel scared, about anything, please tell me," I said. "I can hold you until it passes. That's my job."

We embraced once more before packing up for the night.

CLOSING DOWN THE site was much easier than the initial setting up. With Opal's help, the car was packed in no time. Before leaving, she doused the fire with the remaining half bottle of champagne, celebrating us in her own special way. I tossed the empty bottle in the trash, disposing of the evidence.

When she opened the car door, a fifth rose, a red one this time, lay on her seat. She spotted it right away and clambered into the car to claim the offering. I was rewarded with a kiss after taking my seat. There was something about Opal and roses. From that night on, I never brought her any other type of flower.

* * * * * *

HER PORCH LIGHT was on, welcoming her home. We had five minutes to spare. No matter how badly I wanted to live up to her parents' faith in me, there was no way either of us was going to give up a single minute together. She would be in the house, on time, but not a second before her curfew.

We approached the front door holding hands, wearing devilish grins. To anyone watching, we would have looked guilty as sin. But the only thing we were guilty of was being in love.

Being careful of the thorns, I extracted from my inside jacket pocket the final rose of the night, red. She took a step back and stood, speechless. She thought for a moment as I watched her every blink.

"Five," she said giving count of the red roses. "Why only one white rose?"

"First tell me, which is your favorite?"

"I love the red ones, but I think tonight, I like the white one best."

"That's the reason." I paused, letting it sink in. "You see, tonight is this white rose. I wanted it to stand out amongst all the others. It's the one you won't forget."

She fell into my arms and hugged me hard. Feeling the heat from her body, I looked down and watched her eyes close. I softly said, "You know I love you?"

Keeping a firm grip on me, she said, "Yes, I do. But I think I love you more."

I replied, "Maybe for today, but tomorrow I'll love you even more." And in my heart I meant it.

We kissed goodnight, and she went inside.

AMAZING . . . I had waited my whole life for someone like her, yet, until now, I hadn't realized I was waiting at all. She was more than I could have asked for, more than I deserved.

Love . . .

Ten

Days passed, turning into weeks, and then months. Our so-called friends complained that we had changed. Instead of being happy for us, people seemed jealous and resentful. It was hard to understand why. Though it probably had to do with our world becoming just that, our world, shrunken down to the two of us.

Disapproval came at us from every direction. Opal got pressure from her girlfriends who wanted to spend more time with her. Even her best friend Sandy was "sick and tired" of hearing about me. Opal's parents got in on the act as well. Her mother delivered what amounted to be *the talk*, telling Opal we were getting too serious and needed to slow it down.

My buddies, somewhat less intrusive, made snide comments about being "whipped" and would ask, "When's the wedding?" I ignored it as typical guy banter. My parents, on the other hand, had nothing to say. I'm pretty sure we didn't register a blip on their radar screen. As for my father, Wes, I hadn't spoken to or seen him since the day his certainty stick became useless on me.

Opal and I began to spend less time at the library and more time at her house. We reasoned that less travel would mean more time together. But that plan turned out to have an inherent flaw. From the outset, we became aware that we were never alone. Mrs. Milton was a constant presence and insisted on being a part of our every conversation. Without fail, the moment we finished our homework, she would pop her head into the dining room and interrupt us.

"Kent, would you like something to drink?" she would ask, or "How about a snack?" But my favorite was, "Why don't you two come into the living room and we can all talk?"

It's not like we had a choice, and we understood she had her rights as a parent. But we felt as if we were being watched like criminals on parole for a crime not yet committed.

Though, on the whole, I took the intrusions in stride. Opal didn't seem to mind, so I accepted it, knowing we would have a few minutes alone before I had to leave. Spending time with her, any amount of time, was worth putting up with even her mother. We were in love.

Our conversations with Mrs. Milton generally began on the topic of some current event, school politics, or Mrs. Milton's life philosophy, and then somehow always came around to her declaration that God's plan was at hand. I tended to be guarded, wanting to divulge as little as possible about myself.

Even so, there were occasions when I did reveal more, much more—some of which would have been better left unsaid.

* * * * * *

ONE AFTERNOON, AS we sat at the Miltons' dining room table after finishing our homework, Opal and I were discussing her family tree. I had a sociology assignment to write about my own family, its ancestry and family traits, and knew I was in trouble from the start. Being a child of multiple divorces was bad enough, but add in the deadbeat dads and a few ex-cons in our family tree—Mom's biological father served time for rum-running during Prohibition and his brother had been convicted for manslaughter—and I would have preferred to do the report on someone else's family. Unfortunately, that wasn't an option. The report was worth 80 percent of my grade, and Opal was giving me suggestions on how to write it without revealing certain dark truths. That was when Mrs. Milton came in.

"I hear you're talking about family trees," she said. "Kent, we really don't know much about your family. Maybe you can enlighten us." She used the term "us" a lot, which really meant her. She pulled out a chair and sat, clearly with no intention of going anywhere soon.

For several months I had intentionally dodged questions about my family, but now, backed into a corner, I relented, thinking that perhaps she knew me well enough at this point that I could afford to be more forthright. An uneasy trust had grown between us. Perhaps she wouldn't judge me as harshly as I had imagined.

"Well, where would you like me to start?" I asked.

"How about with your parents?"

"Okay. . . . If you remember, Bernie is my mom's third husband. He's nice and takes real good care of her. We moved to Tustin right after they were married, around four years ago."

"And how many brothers and sisters do you have?"

"It's just the five of us, Mom, Bernie, me, Sissy, and my younger brother, Danny. Oh . . . then I have a half sister on Mom's side, Mary, and Bernie has three sons of his own—so three stepbrothers, and I have another half sister and half brother on my dad's side. . . ." Counting on my fingers, I came up with a number, "Altogether, it's nine kids and a bunch of parents."

When I looked up, I could tell she was disturbed by my answer. Her eyes were wide open, causing her forehead to crease like the bark of an oak tree, rough with numerous folds.

"Sounds like you have a whole lot of family," she said. "Hmmm . . . what about your dad? Do you see him much?"

She had asked me that several times before and knew I didn't see him. The more I thought about it, the more pissed off I got. What was she getting at? She was acting like a cop who kept asking the same questions over and over to see if I'd stick to my story or slip up.

"Nah. . . ." I paused and turned my head so she couldn't see me roll my eyes, and then continued diplomatically, "We don't see eye to eye on things. Actually . . . ," I stopped. That was enough.

"What do you mean?" she asked.

"We've had a few altercations."

"Like what?"

"I'd rather not talk about it," I said, feeling increasingly irritated. I squeezed my hands together under the table so tightly my knuckles turned white.

"That's fine," she conceded. "But I have found that talking about things can help bring about a resolution."

"You really want to know?" I asked, fed up and now defiant.

"Why, yes. But only if you want."

What the hell type of comment is that? I thought. I could tell by her tone that she was dying to know.

"He beat the hell out of me when I was a kid, okay? He kicked the crap out of all of us," I said sullenly, needing to put a stop to the inquisition.

"Oh, my, I see," she said, expressionless. She didn't move, blink, or recoil as if she had stumbled onto a matter too private. Opal, on the other hand, sat with her mouth hanging wide open.

"Do you? Really?" I said defensively. "Mrs. Milton, I know how it sounds. I'm from a two-time broken home, have an abusive father, drive a motorcycle, have long hair, and we don't have a lot of fancy stuff like you do. But underneath, I'm really a good guy." After I'd said it, I wasn't sure who I was trying to convince, her or me.

"Oh, no. Please, you must have misunderstood me," she said. "You are a sweet boy, and we like you very much." Still there was no visible expression of compassion or the slightest nod of understanding. "Well, yes, it does appear that you have had a few unfortunate events in your life. However, you must realize that God gives you only what you can handle. And you've done quite well, considering your circumstances."

I knew she was trying to appease me, but what a load of shit. And then other things I had told her began to come back to me. To start, she wasn't thrilled about the three fights I had been in over the previous six months. Then there was the time I got caught, of all things, stealing a headband when I was twelve. Then in a moment of weakness, I revealed how at the age of thirteen I'd tried to impress my friends by drinking a whole bottle of vodka. I passed out and ended up getting my stomach pumped. The emergency room doctor said I was lucky to be alive—thirty minutes later and I would have died of alcohol poisoning.

If you looked at each event individually, there was a good explanation—okay, maybe not a good one, but justification—I was a dumb-ass back then. And if she were to piece them all together and throw in my family history of broken marriages and violence, then even I wouldn't have allowed Opal to be friends with me. After all, they were an upstanding, churchgoing family. Why should they let their little princess date such an obviously bad influence?

What had I done?

Eleven

From that day on I had an uneasy feeling around Mrs. Milton. There was a subtle shift in her attitude toward me, barely noticeable in our daily interactions. Though she was always scrupulously polite, continuing to offer snacks and drinks, my intuition told me something had changed. However, my perception may have been clouded by the overwhelming desire to spend time with Opal. The ignorance of youth can be a blessing at times.

* * * * * *

THE FOLLOWING FRIDAY night we made plans to double-date with my sister and the new guy. This being their first date, Sissy wanted me to keep an eye on her. The party was supposed to be a rocker with plenty of beer and a band. She intended to keep her wits about herself, as she had a tendency to get carried away, drinking or *smoking it* too much. I was to be her first line of defense—from herself.

Opal's parents were going out, too, which gave me some latitude to bring her home a little later than usual. This was going to be great—more time for just us.

SISSY DROVE, AND the three of us picked up Opal at her house. Her parents had left an hour earlier, taking the three boys with them, leaving the house empty. Of course it crossed my mind—part of me wanted to ditch Sissy and stay right there. Yeah, right, all of me wanted to stay; I was sixteen and a guy. Duh . . .

Resisting the temptation, I walked Opal to the car. She was dressed in a light pink blouse with thin white stripes and bell-bottom Levis. I opened the door to the backseat for her as Sissy lit a cigarette and listened to Elton John's "Harmony" blasting from the radio.

"Bro, you want one?" Sissy shifted around in her seat and held out the pack.

"Nah," I replied.

Opal shot me an admonishing look. "I thought you said you quit."

"I did," I said. "Sissy doesn't know." Opal hated it when I smoked. She said I tasted like an ashtray and couldn't stand kissing me after having one. I needed no other incentive to quit. However, when things got especially bad at home, I would still steal one in here and there. Sissy, on the other hand, enjoyed the whole experience of smoking. Most of her friends smoked, and she wanted to fit in.

"Opal," Sissy said, without looking back. "This is Phil."

Phil, sitting in the front passenger seat, turned around and said, "Hey." Although I'd just met him a few minutes earlier, he seemed like a normal guy. He didn't reek of pot or behave like a jerk. He was polite and open, a pleasant contrast to the long-gone Joe.

Phil was more of an outdoorsman type. He wore a flannel shirt, jeans, and heavy hiking boots. He talked about leaving California for the timberlands of Oregon after graduation. He had dark brown, shoulder-length hair and a chiseled chin, reflecting his Italian heritage. In later years, we would affectionately call him "Skunk" because of the stripe of gray hair that would grow straight down the middle of his head, from his widow's peak to the nape of his neck.

The party was in a house off of Chapman Avenue in the city of Orange, not more than ten minutes from Opal's. We drove slowly past and saw several people hanging out front, smoking and drinking beer. Judging by the look of surprise on her face, I was sure Opal was going to hate it. We parked several streets away and hoofed it to the party.

The house was a typical small, 1930s California bungalow, with large overhangs and a low-pitched roof. The exposed rafters, rustic wood siding, along with the welcoming, broad front porch, were all grounded in the philosophy of the simplicity and practicality of their day.

As we went in the front door, we were each handed a beer. For me, it was no big deal. I took it with a "Thanks." But I kept my eye on Opal, unsure how she would react. She accepted the beer and took a swig like a veteran.

"You okay with this?" I asked tentatively.

"Sure thing, honey," she said happily.

Led Zeppelin played as the beers started to take effect. We danced and drank some more as the smell of pot began to waft through the house. Although only minutes from Opal's house, we were in another city and didn't know anyone else. She stuck close to me. Feeling slightly buzzed, with Opal by my side, I couldn't have been happier. She seemed to be having a great time.

Shots of tequila were being passed around.

"No thanks," I said, remembering my dual purpose that night. I was supposed to keep an eye on Sissy but also wanted to have fun with Opal.

"I'll take one," Opal said.

Quickly downing the first shot, she called for another.

"Sweetheart, you sure you can handle it?" I asked out of concern, starting to feel more like her father than her boyfriend.

"Oh, yeah. I feel sooo gooood." She grabbed the beer from my hand and took a guzzle. Then she threw her arm around my neck.

"You know I love you, right?"

I waved off the girl who was handing out the shots. "And I love you, too," I said.

"Good . . . because you bether," she slurred. "I'm gettin' hot in here."

"Let's go outside and cool off," I suggested.

It was only as I was helping her out the door that I realized she was completely drunk. Not just a little, but a lot, and it was getting worse. The house had filled with partiers, so we sat on the only available spot, the front porch side railing. She teetered as she described how her world was spinning around amidst the murmuring complaints about her mother.

From where we sat, I could keep one eye on Opal and the other on Sissy through a side window. She was standing and talking with Phil and another girl. I waved my arms to get her attention. No luck.

After a couple of minutes, I left Opal to get Sissy. When we got back, Opal was bent over the railing heaving up the tequila and beers into the bushes below.

"You all right, sweetheart?" I asked.

"I'm so sarry. I don't mean to rudin the night. Sarry."

Using her forearm she wiped the drops of undigested alcohol from her chin, then slumped over the railing and retched again.

"Hey, man, you got to take her home," some guy said behind me.

"Yeah, sure thing, dude. Give me a minute," I said. "Sissy, can you drive?"

"No way," she said. "I've had too many beers. But if I have to." She was clearly disappointed to leave.

"Keri, give me your keys," said Phil, taking charge. "Kent, stay with your date. I'll get the car. Nobody go anywhere. I'll be back in two minutes."

THE ENTIRE DRIVE back, I prayed that no one would be home at Opal's. I could see it now: "Evening, Mr. and Mrs. Milton, here's your drunk daughter. Sorry about that. See ya." No, I didn't think so. Whatever the price, short of never seeing her again, I would be willing to shoulder the entire blame. I had resolved myself to taking the hit on this one.

My heart quickened as we turned in to her street and then drove up to the house. The porch light was on, as it had been when we left. There was no way to tell if anyone was home or not. It wasn't even ten o'clock. With Phil's help, I got Opal to the front door and opened it with her key.

"Hello, anyone home?" I called out quietly.

I waited. Nothing.

"Thanks, Phil. I can take her from here," I said, giving him a nod.

He went back to the car.

"Okay, Opal, you're going to have to help me out here," I told her as I picked her up in my arms and rushed up the stairs. Stopping at the top, I asked, "Which way, sweetheart?" I was lost. The upstairs had always been the off-limits zone, another one of her parents' rules.

"Leff. Wow. . . . You're strong."

"Thanks. Which room?"

"There." She pointed and immediately her arm went limp.

Entering the room, I left the light off, not wanting to draw attention to the house. I gently placed her on the bed and hastily removed her shoes and socks.

"Hey, Opal, you're gonna have to put your pjs on and get in bed yourself. Okay?"

"I can't. You do it. Pease?"

Crap, I thought. "Okay, pjs, so where are they?"

"Top drawer. Did I tell youv beefore, earl-ier, I love you? So, so, sooo much. You're pretty hot lookin', too."

My eyes, having adjusted, spotted the dresser in the dark. Opening the far right drawer, I got lucky and immediately found the pajamas and brought them to her.

"And I love you, too. Now please turn around."

As she sat up with her back to me, I pulled her blouse up and off. Quickly placing her arms in the pajama shirt sleeves, I couldn't help but notice the pattern of tiny yellow and orange flowers on her bra. Sadly, I was too nervous to enjoy undressing my girlfriend. Once buttoned, I told her, "Pants."

She flopped back and unbuttoned her pants. With her legs sticking straight up, I yanked them off. She started laughing. I chose to skip the pajama bottoms altogether and helped her get under the covers. Pulling the bedspread up to her shoulders, I kissed her on the forehead.

Rolling onto her side, she said, "I want you to be my first."

I deliberately ignored the remark and quickly folded her clothes into a neat pile. "Good night, sweetheart. I gotta go. I'll call you tomorrow," I said, and headed out the door.

"Don't you want me?" she pleaded from the bed. "I louve you so much. I wanna—to make love to you."

I halted, returned, and knelt by the bed. Staring into her eyes, I said, "Listen, I only have a minute here. You mean everything to me. And, oh yes, god yes, I want you, very much. It'll happen when the time is right. No question about that. Just remember; never, ever forget that I'll love you even more tomorrow."

"I know. Thank you for taking care of me," she said in a little girl voice.

"Always." I kissed her good night and left, locking the front door on my way out.

Got away with one. Maybe?

Twelve

A million thoughts went through my mind. I called the next morning, and her mother said Opal wasn't feeling well, but that she would take a message for her. Then on Sunday, at the risk of making a nuisance of myself, I called twice. No response.

It's funny how your mind can play tricks on you. The lack of a simple phone call can turn your world upside down. My mind raced with wild speculations. Had her parents discovered she was drunk? Did the stench of alcohol and smoke on her clothes give it away? Or had she simply had enough of me?

In my more lucid moments, I didn't give much credence to any of these explanations. But the thought of Mama and Papa Milton discovering their little angel totally inebriated, forever sealing my fate as the bad seed, did weigh on my mind.

I needed to talk to her. It was the not knowing that wreaked havoc on my psyche.

MONDAY MORNING, I left a message in her locker, asking her to meet me at the library that night to talk. Other than occasionally passing each other in the hallways, our schedules kept us apart during school hours. Leaving notes in each other's lockers was a great way to keep each other apprised of the goings on. The messages were usually short on my part, but always ended with "I love you," or, from her, a "Love, Opal" in her rounded, girlish handwriting. We never shared any of the notes or their contents with anyone else; they were part of our private world.

At the end of the school day, with great relief, I picked up her one-word reply: "Ok."

BEING A CREATURE of habit, I was disconcerted to find another couple occupying our usual seats at the library. Glaring at them made me feel better but didn't have the desired effect of getting them to move. They never even glanced in my direction. I reluctantly moved to another table, saving her a seat.

Before I could settle in and spread out, Opal appeared before me, books clutched tightly to her chest. She laid them on the table, her expression revealing nothing.

"Hi," she said timorously.

"Hey. How you feeling?" I asked, trying to be upbeat.

"I wasn't sure if you wanted to talk to me anymore," she said.

"Huh?" I said, baffled, and pointed to the door. She understood.

THE MOMENT WE were outside, I started in. "Why didn't you return my calls?"

"What calls?" she responded as we walked into the parking lot.

"Saturday morning and twice on Sunday. I talked with your mom. You didn't get my messages?"

"No." She stopped and thought for a moment. "Well, Saturday doesn't really count. I was so sick and out of it. I slept the day away. And Sunday . . . well, we went to church and spent most the day out back. She never said anything. I thought you were mad at me."

"Why would I be mad at you?"

She looked down.

"Because I was stupid. I drank too much. Honestly, I don't remember much about Friday night."

I took a step toward her. Reaching out, I lightly brushed her hand with the tips of my fingers. She instantly threw her arms around me and held me close.

"I'm sorry," she cried.

"It's all right," I answered, reassuringly. "I'm just happy you're here."

I filled in the gaps for her, leaving out the bedroom conversation. She asked me how she ended up in bed and if she'd said anything stupid. I told her how I took care of her and tucked her in. I said that she was sweet and kind in spite of being completely toasted. She seemed comfortable, even a little relieved, knowing that I was the one who had seen her in her undies. She was actually more concerned about what she might have said than what she had done.

Secrets . . . bad habits are hard to break.

Thirteen

Yes, I could have said something more, but chose not to embarrass her. The subject of making love would eventually come up again, hopefully sooner rather than later. Of course there had been times when I could have pressed the issue, but I sensed she wasn't ready—we weren't ready—and I deliberately held back. Patience, the virtue she had extolled the first time we met, had become an ingrained part of my character.

Our recent talk at the library exposed much, Opal recognized we had another problem: her mother. She realized that this was not the first time her mother had failed to relay one of my messages. The evidence was mounting, reinforcing my suspicion that Mrs. Milton had it in for me. At least now there was proof.

Newton's Third Law of Motion states, "For every action there is an equal and opposite reaction." In our case, the more her mother tried to keep us apart, the tighter our bond became. In a way, I was glad to have her animosity out in the open.

At first, Opal was upset and then angry. She was determined to confront her mother and have an all-out war over me. I settled her down, and we decided it would be smarter if we kept our mouths shut and our hearts hidden. After all, Mother Milton had the power to make life very difficult for us. Opal agreed that things could be worse. Mother Milton was capable of anything from further limiting her telephone privileges to eliminating our one weekend date night, or even forbidding us from seeing each other altogether. Secure in our devotion, we knew that fending off her mother's interference would be challenging, but manageable. Besides, Mother Milton didn't know what we were capable of.

Tuesday morning was warm with temperatures forecast for the low eighty's. Outside the high school's main gates, she waited. Dressed in shorts, sandals, a loose spaghetti-string top, and backpack in hand, Opal was ready to go. I pulled up in Sissy's car and opened the passenger door from the inside.

"Hey, gorgeous, need a ride?" I flashed my winning smile.

"Sure thing, sailor, but only if you love me," she teased, as she folded herself into the car, tossing the overstuffed bag into the backseat, where it bounced off and then landed on the floor.

"All right," I said, "I'll give you one lifetime. But that's all you get."

She smiled.

We had decided to take the day off and enjoy the beach, our prerogative. We had planned carefully and covered all our bases. I called in sick for her pretending to be Mr. Milton, and she did the same for me as my mom. Opal later remarked that we shared the same kind of sickness—a love bug.

What could go wrong?

WE STOPPED AT Denny's to eat, and within an hour, we were pulling onto Colton Street at the north end of Newport Beach. As I yanked my board off of the car rack, I noticed the streets were unusually deserted for such a warm, sunny day. When the weather was this good, it didn't matter if it was a school day or not—the beach was the place to be.

There were only a couple of tourists on the beach itself. Today it was all ours, just us two. I hit the water and tried surfing for a while, but the waves were small and I eventually surrendered the board in favor of bodysurfing. The water was a brisk fifty-six degrees, so I wore a wetsuit. Opal slathered herself with suntan lotion. A sunburn would have been a dead giveaway.

Later, we lay next to each other, talking and caressing hands. We took a walk along the shore and played in the surf. She shrieked when I kicked up water, splashing her squarely in the small of her back. She tried to return the favor, but I kept dodging her. Seeing she was growing frustrated, I deliberately held up, letting her catch me, and was rewarded for my chivalry with a fistful of wet sand thrown on my back.

But I didn't let her get away with it. I scooped her up and carried her into the waves. She kicked and screamed the entire time, shouting, "Don't you dare drop me. You'll be in big trouble, mister." Yep, into the water she went.

She shot up complaining, "Look at me! My hair . . . I'm freezing."

Actually, I loved what I saw. She was beautiful. Her wet hair was plastered to her cheeks while sand granules adhered everywhere about her skin. I could tell she was cold by her gleaming goose-pimpled skin. Her nipples were erect, protruding through her pink and white bikini top. She came at me with a renewed energy, chasing me down with vengeance in mind.

I beat her to the shoreline, but she was hot on my trail. I turned on her without warning, grabbed her and wouldn't let go. She struggled at first, wriggling madly from side to side, trying to use her brute strength. Finally admitting defeat, she relaxed, and I loosened my grip. She threw her arms around me.

Resting her ocean-soaked hair on my chest, she said, "You do know, when you least expect it . . ."

"Yeah, I know," I said, rolling my eyes, "you'll get me."

"The day's coming, Surfer Boy," she said ominously.

She kissed me anyway.

AFTER OUR MORNING in the sun, we headed back to my place, pleasantly tired, with sand-filled bathing suits. I had planned us a late lunch. As soon as we got home, she wanted to use the bathroom. While I was in the kitchen preparing tuna sandwiches, I heard the sound of running water. I thought we were alone, so the house should have been quiet. I went to investigate, quietly cracking open the bathroom door. Opal stood looking at herself in the mirror, with nothing but a towel wrapped around her.

She caught sight of me in the mirror, and said nonchalantly, as if she had been expecting me, "Yes, can I help you?"

"I'm sorry. I heard the water running and thought someone else was here."

"It was only me. I'm going to take a shower," she said. "And I didn't think you'd mind. You could probably use one, too."

"Yeah, I got a bunch of sand in my hair," I said, throwing back my golden locks.

"Well, get out of here and let me take one," she giggled, slowly closing the door on me.

"Oh . . . yeah," I backed away, getting the message. I waited a moment, listening for the lock to click. It didn't. Convincing myself it was merely an oversight, I went back to the kitchen to make lunch.

As I mixed the mayonnaise into the canned tuna, I imagined myself bursting into the bathroom, tearing off my clothes and jumping into the shower with her. The thought of being naked with her, our skin touching, washing the salt film from her porcelain body excited me to no end. So much so, a pup-tent developed.

"Hey, it's your turn," her voice came from the hallway. "Do you have a shirt I can borrow?"

I turned to face her.

"Wow . . . look at you," she said, her eyes widening.

Uh . . .

Fourteen

Have you ever gotten caught in one of those embarrassing situations? We all have. My brother Danny had to be one of the unluckiest people I ever knew. He got caught for just about everything he ever did wrong and even for things he had nothing to do with. When he was six, he tried to scare these three little girls on our block by taking off all his clothes and running down the street buck naked, screaming. Out of nowhere, the police, who almost never patrolled our block, appeared and picked him up. That was one beating I'll never forget. After all, it was my fault for letting him streak.

Then a couple of years later, believe it or not, he was apprehended by the same cop, for spray-painting graffiti on a wall just around the corner. Mom wasn't thrilled to answer the door to young Danny, spray can in hand, accompanied by Officer Darling.

Another time, he got the bright idea to go up to the roof of a three-story office building and hurl rocks at passing cars. Of course, the first and only car he hit happened to be the sheriff's. Danny and trouble seemed to go like foot in shoe—snug.

And this year, as an eighth grader, he was outdoing himself. What's worse, he had learned to recruit accomplices. Picture this: Danny and a buddy are outside the girls' locker room. Danny talks his friend into letting him stand on his shoulders so he can peer down through the window, trying to spy on the girls as they dress. True to form, before Danny can enjoy so much as a glimpse of bare ass, the principal comes around the corner and walks straight into them, knocking them both to the ground. My brother, poor guy, never could catch a break.

So THERE I was, boner sticking straight out, caught in less than puritanical thoughts. My first impulse was to cover up and turn away, self-conscious of how it must have looked. But instead I decided, why not play it up, making no attempt to conceal my arousal.

"Yeah, see what you did?" I said, hands on hips, showing off. "Getting all naked in my shower—I went crazy at the thought of it."

Opal stared at me as if I were some kind of bizarre specimen. "Well, that's pretty normal, right?" she said tentatively, raising her eyes to meet mine. "So, can I have a T-shirt?"

Her eyes flicked down once more.

"Absolutely," I said, leading her out of the kitchen. "Follow me. Though I gotta warn you, I can't be trusted right now."

She tenderly took my hand.

As I led her down the hall and into the bedroom, my mind filled with erotic fantasies, all of them ending the same way, with her in my arms. I pulled a plain white T-shirt out of my top dresser drawer and handed it to her. As she reached out, her towel came untucked, then unraveled, and slowly fell to the floor, exposing her breasts. She was naked except for a pair of white cotton panties. She didn't flinch, but looked me in the eye without a trace of self-consciousness. The T-shirt slipped from my hands to the floor.

"Can you pick it up for me?" she asked, without shame.

I picked up the towel but, instead of handing it to her, tossed it onto the bed behind me. Trusting my heart, I looked lovingly into her eyes, pulled my shirt over my head, and stepped into her open arms. I wrapped my arms around her. We kissed, lost in the passion of the moment. Experiencing the pleasure of each other's skin, our bodies gave off a tremendous heat emanating from the fervor of our hearts' devotion. Pressing my chest against her bare breasts and feeling her hard nipples fostered a vast increase in my body's excitement. I wanted her. I needed to be with her. She was my world and I hers.

We moved to the bed. We knew our actions were born of pure and true emotion. We were in love.

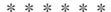

After . . .

SHE CURLED UP next to me, head on my shoulder. I rested my hand on her bare hip. She spoke of our love and said that we'd be together forever and I agreed, wanting nothing more than her, ever.

It's amazing how life can get in the way of living.

Fifteen

I wondered what the hell went through my mind. Why did I even listen when people would say to me, "When you're sixteen you're not supposed to find the one you'll spend the rest of your life with. It doesn't happen. It's not natural."

Or, "This is the time to experiment, to discover what you do or don't like in a girl."

But I already knew what I liked and was lucky enough to have found it. I dismissed their sermons as irrelevant and empty rhetoric. For the most part, their attitudes stemmed from their own failed relationships and had nothing to do with me. Opal and I were different.

* * * * * *

THE LAST DANCE of the year, the prom, was upon us, and I had, of course, asked Opal well in advance and she had immediately accepted. As the date drew near, she grew fidgety with expectation. I assumed it was her usual nerves—she always made a big deal out of the dances and her edginess was par for the course. I knew she enjoyed getting all fancied up, a trait inherited from her mother.

On the night of the dance, she came over to my house early. Mom wanted to take a few pictures of us before the sun went down, "For posterity's sake." I was happy to indulge this rare display of maternal interest. Choosing the front of the house for our backdrop, we stood with our arms around each other. Opal was dressed in a light blue formal gown with a white lace bodice, and panels in a deeper shade of blue up the sides, accentuating her youthful curves. As always, she was radiant. The corsage of three white roses I had pinned on earlier set off the color of her dress and brought out the blue in her eyes. She was simply stunning.

I wore a white tux with a dark blue, ruffled shirt that vaguely matched the darker blue side panels of her dress. As she pinned the boutonniere to my lapel—two white roses with baby's breath—she accidentally pricked me.

"Oh, watch it, babe," was all I said.

Otherwise, the pictures went off without a hitch, and Mom was happy.

We double-dated with another couple, Marty and Cathy. Marty was a senior, a year older than I was. We had met two years before, on the debate team, and had been friends ever since. Girls were attracted to him. With his jet black hair, green eyes, and olive skin, he stood out in any crowd. Though his family didn't have much money and he lived in an older apartment complex, he always seemed to have the latest, coolest clothes. Marty's parents were divorced and his mother had full custody. Both parents showered him with gifts, including a car for his sixteenth birthday. Obviously, they were overcompensating for the guilt of an ugly divorce, and, Marty believed, bidding for his attention. At the time, he was the only other kid I knew who came from a broken home.

Cathy, Marty's date, didn't go to Tustin. She was a Foothill snot. In every city across the nation, you could find a division between the "haves" and the "have nots." She was one of the "haves"—a rich kid from up in the hills who looked down on the rest of us. How Marty had landed her as a date we couldn't figure.

Since Marty was driving, he dictated the ground rules. Actually, there was only one rule: we had to get our own ride home; he and Cathy had plans. His strategy was to leave early and party in a hotel room Cathy had reserved in Newport Beach. We were fine with it, and I had arranged for Mom to pick us up.

Dinner was acceptable—Mexican food at Don José— hard to mess up on beans, lettuce, and tortillas. Cathy droned on about her family's second home up in Lake Arrowhead. She exhausted me with tales of skiing at Brighton, Mammoth Mountain, and Jackson Hole, to name a few. Having never been to any of these places, I found her conversation boring. Other than being a pretty girl with big tits, she didn't have much substance.

What made the dinner tolerable was that we could order drinks from our waiter, who happened to be Cathy's ex-boyfriend. Marty and Cathy each had a Long Island Iced Tea, while I drank a Tom Collins and Opal a Strawberry Margarita. Not wanting a repeat of her last drinking episode, Opal and I were careful to limit ourselves to one drink each. Marty and Cathy partied on.

MARTY DROVE US to the dance, buzzed. We arrived at the school a few minutes past eight, late, and got the last available parking space.

As we walked up to the gym, Marty pulled a flask from his jacket pocket.

"Hey, Kent, want a chug?" he asked.

"No thanks, not tonight," I said.

"Opal, how about you?"

"No, I'm good," she responded, sounding displeased.

"You don't know what you're missing," Marty cajoled.

We both knew. For tonight, all I wanted was to have a little fun, dance, and be with my girl. These were the times I intended to remember.

Once inside the doors, we had to submit to the compulsory registration and then the formal procession to the photo area. I filled out the information card as I eyed the price, knowing I couldn't afford it. Dinner had been cheap, but with the tux rental, tickets and corsage, I was tapped out. We smiled for the photos and moved into the gym.

The gym had been transformed from the cavernous, wood-floored basketball court with stadium-style benches into a blue and white streamer-festooned dance hall. There must have been fifty tables dotting the floor, each decorated with a light blue or plain white tablecloth. The DJ had set up his twin turntables in place of the scorer's table. Several immense speakers provided a huge sound that reverberated through our bodies when the records spun. Opal went directly to an empty table in the back, away from the clamor of the crowd. The dance floor, loosely cordoned off, was full of gyrating bodies, while smaller groups congregated around the refreshment area drinking punch and eating cookies. Few remained at any of the tables.

Marty and Cathy wandered off, and we didn't see them again for the rest of the night. I assumed Marty had danced his one obligatory song, made a quick social round, and left for his real fun.

"Sweetheart, would you like to dance?" I asked. An upbeat song by Chicago was playing.

"Not now. I'd rather just watch for a while," she said. Under her breath I heard her say, "Only with you."

She reached across the table, took my hand, and held it to her cheek. As she stroked the back of my hand, tiny squares of light reflecting off the disco mirror ball danced across her face. She was crying.

"Are you okay?" I asked.

She pulled me toward her.

"Please never forget that I love you," she said earnestly.

"Of course not. And I love you, too."

"No, I mean really. You have to promise me. . . . Promise."

"Okay, I promise." I paused. "What's going on?"

Without replying, she got up and sat on my lap. Avoiding eye contact, she draped her arms around my neck and hugged me. After a few seconds, with a quick kiss on the cheek, she excused herself and went off to the restroom.

When she returned, everything seemed to have gone back to normal. She smiled and appeared happy to be there. We danced, drank punch, and laughed.

Something always brought her back to me.

Sixteen

The last dance of the night was traditionally a slow song, and we weren't disappointed. The opportunity to hold her was one thing I never passed up. Stealing her away from her friends, I pulled her onto the dance floor. She clutched my left hand and immediately rested her head on my chest. I felt the warmth of her body as we swayed to the music, dancing as if we were the only two in the gym. I didn't know the song or who sang it, and I didn't really care. We were together and that's what was important. As the song approached its final chords, her arms tightened around me. She clung to me with such ferocity that I felt that she was trying to tell me something. I held her, wishing the music would never end, bent my head to her ear, and gently whispered, "I love you." Her arms tightened even further.

The song ended.

WE SLOWLY WALKED to the pay phones outside the administration building and I grudgingly called Mom to come pick us up. It left us with a few minutes to kill, so we strolled back into the school's main quad area. We found a bench in a dimly lit section and sat for a moment, gazing at each other. It was the perfect place to be alone and share a few kisses. I remembered it was here where I had seen her for the first time, all dressed up in her Sadie Hawkins outfit.

I leaned in, but instead of our lips meeting, she moved her head to one side and gave me a peck on the cheek.

What the hell is that? I thought.

"Hon, wait," she said. Pulling away from me, she continued, "We need to talk. Um . . . I need to talk." She looked down at her feet.

"What's the matter?" I asked.

"I'm not sure how to tell you this. . . ." She looked sad.

"Go ahead, what is it?"

"I think we need to break up."

"What? Oh, come on," I said, certain it was a joke.

"No, really. I have to break up with you," she said more firmly.

I slid down the bench, creating more than just a physical distance between us. I looked at her in amazement. Her eyes remained fixed on the ground.

"What?" I repeated.

"I'm sorry," she said.

Stunned, I stood up, trying to shake off the words I had just heard. I couldn't believe it. I narrowed my eyes and heard my voice rise, seemingly of its own volition.

"Why? And what about us?" I argued.

She stood, clearly upset herself, her eyes beginning to fill with tears.

"I'm sorry to hurt you, but I have to end it," she said, her voice cracking.

I turned my back on her. All I felt in that moment was anger. But soon panic crept in, and the reality that there might no longer be an us terrified me. With what little composure I had left, I asked again, "But why?"

"Because I have to . . . ," she pleaded. There was a long pause. "I like someone else."

"You like someone else?" Turning to face her, my voice grew louder. "What do you mean, you like someone else? That's a load of shit. And don't tell me you don't love me anymore, 'cause that's a lie, too!"

She didn't respond. I stared. Her face was expressionless, yet tears streamed down her cheeks. She didn't look me in the eye. She couldn't.

"Fine, let's go," I said, sounding detached. I felt nauseated and wanted to hit someone.

Silently, I suppressed my gag reflex, ignoring her as I walked to the pick-up spot. At that point, I didn't care if she was following or not. In fact, I hoped she would find her own ride home. But in my peripheral vision, I saw she was right on my heels.

THE WAIT FOR my mother felt like an eternity. I didn't dare look at her for fear I would do something stupid or cause a scene I'd later regret. Feeling her eyes burning holes into me, I now avoided her stare.

"Hey, Kent, Opal, nice dance, huh?" Kevin, my friend, spoke as he walked up with his date, Linda.

"Sure," I said, giving the shortest answer possible, having no desire to talk.

"We saw you two on the floor at the end. You guys always look so happy," said Linda. "It's great to see a couple like you two."

"Thank you. You're very kind," Opal chimed in with her usual candy-coated speech. I wanted to puke.

At that moment, Mom drove up. I opened the car door for Opal, pretending all was right in the Opal-Kent world, knowing the rumors would start soon enough. With a half-assed wave to Kevin and Linda, I reluctantly got in and sat beside her.

THE DRIVE TO her house was worse than I could have imagined. The tension between us was heavy, filled with anxiety, uncertainty, and despair. No one spoke, apart from my mom who asked about the dance. I remained silent, leaving Opal to answer her questions in her polite and insincere manner—of course excluding the part where she'd dumped my ass.

I wanted her gone. We pulled up to her house, and as I opened her door I saw her eyes welling up. I couldn't handle it. I hated to see her cry, but the thought of talking to her right now was out of the question.

I walked her up to the first step.

"Thank you for the dance," she said, as teardrops fell upon her cheeks and lips. She reached out to touch my arm.

I took two steps back, "Yeah, sure," I said, and turned and walked away.

SAFE IN THE car, I didn't wave goodbye or watch her go into the house. I sat motionless, petrified. Mom asked me a question. I didn't hear it. Instead, I made a single statement.

"Opal broke up with me tonight, and I don't want to talk about it."

I looked out the window, avoiding the sympathetic stare in the rearview mirror. My face remained vacant with the exception of a blink here and there, each one releasing a tear.

Dreams are for sleeping, not for real life.

Seventeen

The morning after that horrific night . . . I was broken, soulless. My heart had been shattered. Everything I had believed in, the one person I had loved and trusted the most—gone. I was numb—if I had any sensation at all. Crushed.

Sleeping but a few hours, I found myself in the garage, sitting in a beach chair, garage door wide open, listening to America's "Homecoming" album and then switching back and forth to selected songs from Elton John's "Captain Fantastic and the Brown Dirt Cowboy." For privacy, I kept the music turned down low, allowing me to wallow in uninterrupted self-pity. The songs' sweet melodies seemed only to intensify my grief, but I didn't really want to feel better anyway.

I searched for, and finally found, a pack of cigarettes stashed in Sissy's glove compartment, tucked in between a sheaf of papers and the car's maintenance guide. I tried to smoke away the pain. The questions repeated themselves in an endless loop in my brain. None of it made any sense. How could I have lost her to someone else? What had I done wrong? I thought we were fine. What happened? Each time, every time, I came up empty. I had no answers.

Shrouded in cigarette smoke with bloodshot eyes, I was once again alone. No longer would she be there for me, listening to what I had to say, or discussing the plans we had made together. What's more, because she was my greatest confidante, it was she I would have turned to in a crisis. Now, in the midst of the worst heartbreak of my life, I had no one. Not only had I lost my first love, but also my best friend.

I lit another cigarette.

Even though my eyes were closed tight, shadows still existed.

Hope...

Eighteen

Tick-tock, tick-tick, tick-tock. It's hard to see the hands move when you're watching the clock.

The month that followed saw the end of the school year and the beginning of summer. Each day the pain lessened, but my love for her lingered just below the surface. I spent the first weeks of summer surfing every morning; up at five, on the water by six, trying to ease the joylessness of what I called my life. Then it was off to work by eight.

I was fortunate to have been hired by my neighbor, Scott's father, Mr. C., as he liked to be called. Living across the street from them had paid off. He had watched me over the years and never expressed an opinion on my long hair or the rancid smell of smoke wafting from my clothes. He simply requested I be on time and "put in an honest day's work" and we wouldn't have any problems. Mr. C. was a good man, forthright and honest, and at times I was envious of Scott's relationship with him.

As the sole owner and operator of The Crow's Nest, a ship and yacht brokerage, Mr. C. hobnobbed with some of Newport Beach's wealthiest. The business was located on the Newport Peninsula's harborside in a refurbished fish-packing plant. His inventory included several new Ranger sailboats, from the smaller 23-foot boat to the pricy 37-footer. Behind the warehouse, The Crow's Nest rented several docks from the city where the more expensive yachts were berthed.

My job was basic maintenance on all of the boats: washing the decks, polishing the chrome railings, cleaning the bilges, and scrubbing the exterior hulls, including those of the yachts in the harbor, once a week. Although any monkey could have done my job, I found the mindless labor therapeutic. And the best part about it—on my better days, I was so physically exhausted I didn't have the energy to think about her.

Typically before leaving work, I would check on my surfboard to make sure it hadn't been moved during the day. Since I couldn't transport it on my motorcycle, I stored it in the back corner of the building, away from the doors so it wouldn't get stolen, yet with easy access for my early morning surf. Once reassured that the board was still there, I would linger, striking up a conversation with whoever was left on the floor. The truth was I didn't want to go home.

At home, particularly at night, I was miserable. I was forced to be with me, alone with my thoughts. Whenever the phone would ring, I would pick up, silently praying it was her, but it never was. You would think after the hundredth time—and no Opal—I would have learned. No, not me. In spite of everything, especially not having spoken to or seen her since that night, I kept hoping. I still believed in us, beyond all reason.

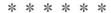

FINALLY, HAVING HAD enough of this quest for self-destruction, I decided to take action. So on that next Saturday, I went looking for advice from an old friend. Linda lived one street over from me, and had called earlier in the week just to say hi. I thought I would pay her a visit, hoping she could provide a different perspective on my situation. She and Kevin had been dating for some time and idolized Opal and me as a couple. When she heard about our breakup, she made of a point of telling me she was a good listener if I ever needed someone to talk to.

She was a good-hearted, no-agenda type of girl—a rarity. It felt strange talking to her about Opal. Actually, it felt strange talking to anyone—other than Opal—about anything. Linda listened and then gave me her opinion: I had to talk with Opal in person, now, "one way or another."

THE NEXT THING I knew, I was standing on the sidewalk in front of Opal's house. Judging from appearances, everything was the same. The grass was cut short, the hedges that lined the property were squared off and clear of debris, and the Mercedes-Benz parked in the driveway gave an indication that someone was home. I was sure the roar of the motorcycle had announced my arrival.

As I made my way up the front walk, I had an attack of nerves. Suddenly, I couldn't remember a time when I hadn't been nervous in this place. My stomach churned as I knocked on the front door. I heard her voice on the other side of it, and my heart began to race. The door opened. It was her.

"Hello, Opal," I said. She slammed the door shut. I stood facing the wood panels, stunned, mouth hanging open.

I heard her voice again, and then her mother's screeching tone. When she spoke, it reminded me of the Wicked Witch of the West. Their conversation went on for what seemed like several minutes. I couldn't make out what they were saying. Finally, the door swung open again, and Mother Milton stood in the doorway with Opal behind her. Opal's eyes were red, as if she had been crying.

What had I just stepped into? By her scowl it was obvious Mother Milton wasn't happy to see me. This may have been a really bad idea. But I was still hurting and had to talk with Opal.

"Please come in, Kent," Mother Milton said icily, stepping aside for me.

As I crossed the threshold, a sudden chill spilled down my spine like a cat's back hair will stand on end, follicles electrified, in a defensive mode.

"Thank you," I said.

"We're surprised to see you," Mother Milton said, "but, exactly why are you here?"

Damn . . . I'm right, this is a bad idea, I thought.

"Ma'am, I wanted to talk with Opal. It shouldn't take long."

"Apparently we have another problem right now, son," she said, still in that icy tone.

"Ma'am?" I said, innocently.

"A little over an hour ago we received a phone call telling us you were in an accident. We were getting ready to come see you at the hospital."

"What?" I looked at the both of them in surprise. Opal wiped away a tear with a Kleenex, composing herself but remaining in her mother's shadow.

"The caller said you were in Hoag Hospital with a broken leg," Mother Milton went on. "She identified herself as your sister."

"It was Keri," Opal spoke for the first time.

"No, come on," I addressed Opal, flatly rejecting the idea.

"Well, it sounded like her, and then here you are out of the blue. What kinda trick are you playing on me?" Opal said, crying through her words.

"I honestly don't know what's going on," I pleaded. "I just wanted to talk with you, that's all. I need—I wanted to—to clear things up."

"And it happens to be on the same day we get this call?" said Mother Milton suspiciously. "Kent, this doesn't sound right." She frowned.

"Did she say her name was Keri?" I asked Opal directly.

"I think so. Or . . . or maybe she said, 'This is Kent's sister.' I'm not sure exactly."

"I'm sorry, but until I talk with Sissy, I don't know what to say. . . . And if she has anything to do with this, I will kill her," I added angrily.

"Hmmm . . . ," Mother Milton paused. "Well, the most important thing is you're okay. Though maybe you should go." It was more of a directive than a suggestion.

"Yes, ma'am," I said, but then stopped. "Would it be all right if I spoke with Opal for a minute?"

Mother Milton clenched her jaw; I saw a vein pop out of her neck. Opal looked terrified.

"Okay, but only for a minute," she said.

OPAL FOLLOWED ME onto the front porch, leaving the door open. Mother Milton remained within earshot. Keeping my distance, I turned to Opal and asked, "Do you have any idea why anyone would do this?"

Of course, what I was really thinking was how it would feel to have her in my arms again. She looked gorgeous. Tanned, with sun-lightened hair, no doubt she had been spending time at the beach.

"No, I don't," she said.

"Why are you crying?" I asked as another tear rolled down her cheek.

"Because I really thought you were hurt . . . and . . . ," her words trailed off, "and I forgot what I did to you."

Did I hear her right? Was it possible she still cared? I knew Mother Milton was eavesdropping on every word and this was one subject not for her ears.

"Listen," I said, "I don't want to talk about that right now. First let me speak with Sissy and see what she knows. Can I call you later and tell you what I find out?"

"Yes, but not too late, though," she said, taking a quick peek back at her mother. She smiled and hugged me, which took me by surprise, and gave a wave as she went back inside.

Hope is the soul of any wish.

Nineteen

I slammed the front door behind me and yelled, "Keri Ann, where are you?" I knew she was home because her old '64 Plymouth Valiant was parked out front.

Her room was located immediately to the left of the front door, so she could hear every footstep in and out of the house. She came out of her room.

"Lower your voice, would you," she said. "I'm right here."

She knew I was pissed off about something when I called her Keri Ann. "What's your problem?"

"Why'd you call Opal?" I barked.

"Opal who? What, your old girlfriend Opal? What would I call her for?" she said, staring me down.

"So, you didn't call her and tell her I was in the hospital?" I demanded.

"No. Get real," she said scornfully.

"Well, someone called her and said I was in an accident and was down at Hoag Hospital."

"Don't be an idiot. And why would I do that anyway?"

"That's what I'm asking you. So, where were you today?"

"I worked all day." She scrunched her nose at me.

"The caller said she was my sister. Plus Opal said she recognized your voice."

"Be serious, Kent," said Sissy, exasperated. "I didn't call her. And if I did, why would I leave my name or say I'm your sister? Now that would be pretty thick, wouldn't it?"

"Oh . . . yeah, that makes sense."

"Since you're supposedly so smart, try using some common sense. The caller was a girl, right?" she went on.

"Yeah . . ."

"Then it's probably a girl you both know. Maybe someone who has it in for you—or her. I don't know or care. But don't go blaming me."

"Uh. . . ." I had to relent. Having nothing left to say except "Sorry," I went off to my room to brood.

I LAY ON my bed and decided to wait a while before calling Opal. I didn't want to appear overzealous, even if I was.

* * * * * *

THREE HOURS AND thirty minutes to the second later, I left.

NEEDING TO GET out and wanting some privacy, I walked to the Pac Bell building two blocks away. A pay phone hung on the brick wall just outside the building's entrance. I had used this pay phone many times before and could talk as long as I liked for my dime. I deposited the coin and dialed her number.

"Hello, Opal?" I asked, even though I recognized her voice.

"I was hoping it was you," she said, sounding genuinely glad to hear from me. "So . . . what did you find out?"

Her tone was sweet and welcoming. I savored every syllable, grateful to hear that voice again on the other end of the line.

"Sorry, but it wasn't Sissy," I said recounting the conversation with my sister.

"Then who would do this to me? To you?"

"The caller was a girl, right?" I said, repeating Sissy's logic.

"Yeah."

"And it's probably someone who knows both of us. Do you know of anyone who would want to screw with you by using me?" I asked.

"Only one of your ex-girlfriends," she replied snidely.

"Oh come on, Opal," I said, disappointed. "That's not helping."

"I'm sorry. I'm just upset. All I could think about was you being hurt, in a hospital bed, and it scared me." She paused and I waited for her to continue. "I was sad. You have no idea what went on in my head."

"No more scared than I was when your mom said, 'Kent, we have a problem.' She looked like she wanted to rip my head off. Actually, I thought she was going to say, 'You need to leave and don't come back. You're not welcome here any longer.'"

"No, no—she was just upset too," Opal interjected. "It was bad for the both of us. We were ready to leave for the hospital when you knocked. My parents do like you."

"I'm glad someone in your family does," I said, half joking.

Then it became quiet on her end, which turned into an awkward silence—no sigh or giggle—not even the sound of her breath. The faint buzz of the telephone was suddenly very loud in my ear. The paralyzing silence persisted. I began to wonder if she was still there.

Finally, she said, "I don't expect you to forgive me. And I don't know if you will believe me or not, but I still care for you."

I couldn't believe my ears. Had she really said she still cares? To my surprise, I became wary of her words, unsure of their meaning. I chose to keep my distance.

"Kent, are you going to say something?"

"Listen, Opal, it's getting late. Can I call you tomorrow?" I asked, anxious to get off the line.

"You sure you will?" she pleaded.

"Sure, yeah, I will. Oh . . . again, sorry I couldn't help much."

"I'm just happy you're okay," she said, and I almost believed her.

"Thanks. Talk to you tomorrow."

"Good night," she said sweetly and hung up.

Memories are cruel. The desire to relive them can be worse.

Twenty

That night I slept better than I had in a long time. I awoke feeling good for a change and looked forward, of all things, to spending Sunday painting the house. Mind you, not the entire house, but the trim and other wood accents. Though our house was on the smaller side and mostly covered in stucco, I still figured it would take me the better part of the day to get it done.

I unwound the extension cord and plugged it into the electrical outlet and guided the orange flex-cord out and around the garage, up the L-shaped front walkway leading to front door. I plugged in the radio and turned the dial until I found a song I liked—David Bowie's "Space Oddity," a hit song from a few years earlier that fit my mellow mood. Returning to the garage, I gathered the basic tools: a gallon can of exterior acrylic brown paint, a flat-head screwdriver to pry open the can, roller pan, roller, and two paint brushes. Holding the paint can in both hands, I shook it vigorously.

Somewhere between opening the paint and pouring its dark brown contents into the rolling pan, thoughts of Opal seeped into my mind. I deliberately pushed them out and tried to concentrate on getting enough paint onto the brush for the long precise strokes required. But thoughts of yesterday's encounter and last night's phone call kept creeping back in, and I eventually stopped fighting them.

By the way our conversation ended, much was left unresolved. Two weeks earlier, I would have given anything just to hear her voice. I loved the way it rose an octave or two when she got excited or how soft it became when we were cheek to cheek. She had caught me off guard, asking me, it seemed, for forgiveness and then telling me that she still cared for me. I had frozen, and I knew it. The moment she opened up, my defense mechanisms kicked in. I reverted to my old self, guarded and emotionally removed.

How else was I supposed to react? She was the one who had crushed me. All I could think of was how it had felt that night, and in an instant the pain resurfaced, neither forgotten nor forgiven. I wanted to hate her. Yet, even after all that had happened, what I felt was on the opposite side of that line of hate.

So I painted the house, contemplating my options, stopped at an emotional fork in the road. Part of me wanted to move on, to remember the good we shared, to take what I had learned and try again with someone new. All logic and intellect pointed me toward turning the page on this chapter of my life.

But on the other hand, there was another part of me that wanted to take a chance, to try to recapture some of the passion we once had. The fact was that I had never stopped thinking about her. Time had passed and yet I was more in love with her each day.

I knew the answer. After all, there was no one there to protect me from what I wanted.

* * * * * *

As THE SUN set, I was finishing up. I looked down at the three empty paint cans at the foot of the ladder and felt a sense of accomplishment. I had painted the trim and made a decision about Opal. As I climbed down the ladder for the last time, I heard Mom call out my name.

"Yeah, Mom, I'm around the corner," I yelled back.

"Can you put down whatever you're doing?" she said in a strict, cold tone. "We need to talk," she said even more ominously.

"Sure thing, I'll be in, in a minute."

"No, I mean now!" she demanded.

Oh, crap, what have I done now, I thought to myself.

I put down the brush and wiped myself off with a rag, blotting up any errant paint spots. When I came in the front door, I found everyone sitting in the living room—Bernie on the couch next to Mom, and Sissy beside Bernie, weeping. My brother Danny appeared from his bedroom and we both sat on the floor staring up at Mom, who looked completely frazzled.

"Boys, I'm afraid I have some bad news," she said. "Your grandmother just called. Grandpa's dead."

My ears heard . . .

Twenty-one

Was life really supposed to be like this? So much pain, heartbreak, death?

GRANDPA HAD DIED in his sleep, leaning back in his favorite recliner, watching television. He had been taking a nap before dinner, never to wake. At seventy-two, he had lived several lives, all of them arduous and harsh. Despite his station in life, he always said, "What is right, is right." Grandpa Heil was the only positive male role model in my life.

When I was a child, he'd treated me differently from his other grandkids. Perhaps because I was the first boy, the son he never had. Or perhaps because of the summers I spent helping him in the shop. Or it could have been because he knew a secret about me, one he never revealed, and loved me especially because of it. Even years later, I never found my answer, which only reinforced our family motto: secrets.

After the initial shock wore off, after the questions and sadness, all I could think of was her. I needed Opal.

* * * * * *

MOTHER MILTON ANSWERED the phone.

"Hello, is Opal there?" I asked. In the depths of my grief I was immune to her disapproval.

"Just a moment please. Who's calling?" she asked, knowing full well it was me.

"This is Kent, ma'am," I said politely, being two-faced.

"Oh, I see. Opal, it's for you," she said frostily.

"Hello," came Opal's voice.

"Hey. It's me."

"I'm glad you called," she said, sounding relieved.

"Can I come over? I need to talk to you. It's really important." My voice cracked.

"Let me ask," she said and put down the receiver.

I heard voices, and then she came back on the line.

"It's okay," she said. "Come on over, but Mom said only for a short time."

"Thanks. I'll be there in five minutes," I said and hung up.

I RUSHED OUT of the house, my hands, hair, and clothes speckled in paint, leaving the empty paint cans out front, ladder still leaning against the house, and several brushes left out drying.

Within minutes, I was once again knocking on her front door. Opal answered and invited me in. I didn't move.

"Can you come outside? I'm filthy," I said.

She stepped onto the porch, and I couldn't hold it in any longer. I grabbed her and held her as the tears poured out. My body started to shake with sobs, and it was only then that she realized I was crying.

"What's wrong?" she asked.

"Grandpa died tonight," I said, shaking.

She didn't let go of me or say anything. She just held onto me and let me cry. In that quiet space, I felt safe. She understood without explanation or reason. Between us, nothing had changed.

"I'm so sorry," she said at last, releasing me as she felt my grip loosen.

Now facing her, my hand slid down from her shoulder to her hand. "Opal, I don't want to do this anymore," I said. "I miss you. I miss my best friend. Are we really done?"

She took two steps back and then turned away. Her hands went to her face, and I heard her sniffle, followed by three or four heavy breaths. I expected the worst. But until she looked me in the eye and told me so, I refused to believe it was over.

"Did you hear me?" My voice rose. "Turn around and tell me." Tears rolled down my cheeks, and anger, grief, and confusion roiled in me all at once.

"What, you're afraid of hurting me?" I went on, even louder. "It's too late for that . . . so tell me to my face."

"Is everything okay out here?" Mother Milton appeared at the doorway, drawn by my raised voice. She came out onto the porch and saw Opal in tears, then directed her focus to me.

"Son, you're a nice boy. Don't you think it's time to let her go?" Her tone was one of restrained anger, but her eyes were filled with hatred, giving her away.

"No, I don't!" I was shouting now, furious. "And you can't decide for us when or if it should end. That's our decision and ours alone, so just stay out of it!"

Opal looked at her mother and said through tears, "I can't. I still love him."

She ran past me into the house.

Twenty-two

I left.

I WENT DIRECTLY to the U-Tote-Em store and bought a pack of Marlboro Reds. I drove to the base of a small hill off La Colina Drive, parked, and trekked a couple of hundred yards up the dirt path to the top. Sitting on the lone rock at the summit, I lit a cigarette and cried for the loss of Grandpa. I began to wonder what the fallout would be from my mouthing off to Mother Milton. Did any of this really matter? Overlooking the city of Tustin, I felt small and insignificant.

When I got home, I found a message next to the phone that Opal had called. It was too late to call her back. In any case, I had had all that I could deal with for one day. Mom came out of her room to see who'd come in. She sniffed me as I walked by, picking up the reek of smoke. She gave me *the look* declaring her disapproval but said nothing. She knew I was managing things in my own way. To her credit, the one thing she did right as a mother was to leave us kids alone when it came to issues of the heart. Besides, she was in her own hell, coping with the loss of her stepfather, and there would have been no point in burdening her with my pain. It's not like she could have helped. So, I kept it to myself as I always did.

* * * * * *

MONDAY MORNING, I called Mr. C., and he gave me the week off to mourn. It was nice of him, but I knew I wouldn't be able to handle an entire week at home alone with all that time to think.

Mom had left for San Diego earlier that morning to take care of the funeral arrangements. Grandma was a mess and needed Mom with her. Bernie took care of things at home, doing the cooking but not much else. Danny and Sissy were in and out, mostly spending time with their friends. They didn't like being home either. Mom scheduled the funeral for Friday afternoon, meaning we would have to leave Thursday morning to arrive in time for the viewing.

I had to get out of the house. I returned Opal's call and made plans to meet her at the elementary school playground near her house, adjacent to the Presbyterian church.

She wanted to talk, too. Realizing this could very well be our last conversation, I had made a decision. This state of limbo I was living in would have to end today.

OPAL WAS SITTING on a swing and raised her head when she heard me pull up on the motorcycle. A smile briefly crossed her lips as she stood up to greet me. I kicked the stand down and walked toward her, helmetless, my hair blown back from the ride. I was ready.

We stood on the grass, five feet apart, which felt more like five miles.

"You wanted to talk," I said. "So where're we at?"

"You first," she said.

"Screw this." I turned to go.

"What, you're not man enough to tell me what you feel?" She was yelling. "Come on, Surfer Boy, I know you heard me last night!"

I turned around to face her.

"Damn it, Opal," I said, "do you want me or not?"

"I never wanted anything so much," she said, crying, and ran into my arms. I held her. "I love you," she whispered. "Please don't go. Stay. It's always been you."

To give oneself fully, without pride or self-consciousness, with a pure heart, is a rare thing. She hadn't held back in the face of my intransigence. I surrendered.

"Oh, Opal, I've missed you," I murmured into her hair.

She kissed me.

"Don't you ever do that. . . ." She paused, then kissed me on my neck. "Don't you ever leave me."

We kissed again.

"I understand if you're angry; take however much time you need to forgive me. I'll be here," she said with conviction.

"I don't need any time," I answered instantly. "Look at me," I said, taking her by the shoulders. "I mean, really look at me. Do you see it? Do you recognize it? This is what love looks like."

"Yes," she said. "I've always known it. Oh, how I love you."

We kissed and held each other for what seemed like hours. Forgiveness, healing, denial, or whatever it was, we never discussed the night of the dance nor the other guy she had supposedly left me for. The words that she once had put between us no longer existed. We did speak of the irreparable rift I had opened up with her mother. Plainly stated, Mother Milton couldn't stand me. She was convinced that her daughter could do better. But Opal was adamant that from now on she was going to do what she wanted, and that included being with me. We were together again, against life's prevailing surge of objections. Our love blossomed.

Love is never lost, only covered up by layers of time.

Twenty-three

The next five weeks were some of the happiest of my life. We saw each other every day, except Sundays, of course. Shockingly, her mother was accommodating, allowing Opal to spend more time with me. Was this a bad omen?

Anytime when things were going too well, I had learned not to trust it. It was only a matter of time before all hell broke loose. At least, that's how it had always been for me.

Hell broke loose . . .

I got a frantic call from Opal before evening had settled in. We had plans to meet within the hour, but she insisted it couldn't wait. She wouldn't elaborate, and her voice cracked several times. I left right away.

When I drove up, she was sitting on the porch swing. She jumped up and met me halfway down the walk, throwing her arms around me without a word. Her eyes were bloodshot and her hair messy. Right then I knew something was horribly wrong. She led me back to the swing and we sat.

"There's something I have to tell you," she said, then paused and looked down, grabbed my hands and held onto them tightly. She started to cry, tears dripping onto her lap, soaking into her cotton shorts. I had seen her cry before, but never like this. These were tears of true sadness. My heart broke for her.

"What is it, sweetheart?" I implored. "Whatever it is we can fix it together," I said confidently.

"You can't fix this. I can't fix it either," she wept.

I folded her into my arms and held her. "Sure we can," I said gently.

"I've been dreading this day. I prayed it would never happen. We're moving."

"What?" I was stunned and pulled back.

"We're moving. And . . . and we're leaving on Saturday." Only then did she look up and into my eyes.

"Saturday," I said. "That's in two days! No. Where?"

"London. Dad took an assignment there, and we're really going." She fell against me, sobbing uncontrollably.

I was dumbstruck. This wasn't happening. She couldn't leave. No. "There's got to be something we can do," I pleaded.

"Nothing . . . and it gets worse," she said between muffled sobs.

"Worse? How could it?"

"Tonight's the last time I can see you. Tomorrow we pack, and Saturday we leave early in the morning."

"No, no, no frickin' way," I moaned. "This isn't right. How can they do this?"

"Please stop. Honey, there's nothing you can do. I argued with them for hours. It's happening."

"So, what, you want me to just give up and let you go? I can't. I won't." Tears didn't come, only anger.

She grabbed my hands again, clutching them firmly. "Listen, listen," she begged. "We have to. Please, don't make it harder than it already is. I love you so much. Please don't." She continued to cry.

I felt lost. Apart from kidnapping her on the spot, what could I do? I wanted to run, to cry. What was going to happen to us? I was overcome with a terrible, daunting dread.

"Let's go for a walk," she said.

SOME DISTANCE FROM her house, we crossed 17th Street and staggered into the Trinity United Presbyterian Church parking lot, holding each other up like a couple of drunks. I gripped her hand so tightly I was afraid I might break it. Every ten steps or so, we stopped and kissed, and she continued to weep.

Then she said, not out of meanness, not in anger, but in a whisper so her voice wouldn't crack, "We have to end us—tonight."

"No. Why?" I said, astonished.

"Honey, think."

"I know. You'll be thousands of miles away. But we can write and . . ."

"And what? It's not like I'm coming back anytime soon."

"Yeah, but . . ."

"Kent, no, please help. This is hard enough. My heart is breaking, and I need your support."

Wanting to be strong for her, I agreed. We held each other. She cried, but my eyes remained dry.

KNOWING SHE WAS right, everything we had started to slip away from me. The walk back to her house was excruciating. She said she wouldn't write, and I understood that she couldn't. She cared for me too much to continue hurting me. Her tears streamed down as we got closer to her house. It was time.

We kissed with as much passion as we had ever done in our lives, neither of us wanting to stop. Ultimately, it was she who broke off the kiss and then held me tightly.

"I love you with all my heart. Always have and always will," she said through sobs.

"I love you more," I answered.

"Only in your dreams, Surfer Boy."

I gave her a final kiss and a hug and said goodbye. I drove off, waving, leaving her standing on the sidewalk, hands over her mouth, crying. That's when my tears started.

* * * * *

I NEVER CALLED on Friday to say goodbye, nor did she. It was over.

The penance for my youth's innocence was paid in full.

Part II

A new life, same old feelings . . .

Twenty-four

❦

Five years passed.

It was Friday, three weeks before Christmas. In four months, I would be graduating from UCLA. I looked forward to moving from Los Angeles back to the Orange County area. As always, the Friday night traffic heading south on the 405 Freeway was horrendous. It felt like the speedometer never went above fifteen miles per hour. By the time I got there, it was always later than I had hoped, and tonight was no different. But that's the price I paid whenever I came home for the holidays, vacations, or to house-sit. This time, it was a double dipper— Christmas break and house-sitting for Mom and Bernie while they went to look after my Great Aunt Eleanor.

Now that all the kids were grown and Grandma Heil had died, too, Mom and Bernie had taken on the responsibility for seventy-four-year-old Eleanor. She was Mom's last living relative, and Mom felt a sense of obligation to her. Over the previous three years, Eleanor's health had deteriorated rapidly, and her dependency on my parents increased. She had recently undergone hip replacement surgery, and Mom and Bernie had left that morning for Phoenix. They were expecting to be gone at least three weeks.

Actually, I didn't mind. I looked forward to the peace and quiet. It would be a break from the hectic pace of school, fraternity, work, and my latest girlfriend, Diana. I could use the time to relax, get away from everyone, and maybe even catch up on some sleep. I had intentionally neglected to give anyone my contact number, including Diana. I would call her when I was ready. Not that I didn't care for her, but after dating her for three months, I had come to realize that we each wanted different things. She wanted me, and I didn't want her.

When Opal moved, I found myself either not dating at all or jumping from one relationship to the next without establishing any real connection. After we said our final goodbyes, I didn't see or even talk to another girl the first year and a half. Once the heartbreak and loneliness eventually faded to a tolerable level, I became, for lack of a better term, a player. But somehow every relationship that began with such hope and mutual attraction would ultimately fail for one reason or another. Was it that I compared each girl to Opal? Or maybe I was on some self-destructive mission to end up alone? Regardless, in the end, each relationship was doomed, and the only common denominator was me. Sadly for Diana, our relationship was headed in the same dismal direction.

The house was dark as I drove up, no porch or any other light illuminated. My parents had moved to Villa Park three years ago. The house and neighborhood were a substantial step up from the place in Tustin. This house was twice the size and very roomy for a single-story, ranch-style dwelling. The grounds were nicely landscaped including a pool and Jacuzzi in the backyard. I was proud of them for having finally made it; at long last they had achieved a modest piece of the American pie. After the many years of financial struggle, they had been rewarded for their diligence, perseverance, and mostly risk. During the California real estate boom, they had bought and sold several properties and then sunk it all into this new place. Unfortunately, since I no longer lived at home, I wasn't a beneficiary of their good fortune, apart from the occasional free meal and a place to stay.

I unlocked the front door, flipped on a light, and threw my backpack onto the dining room table. After a couple of trips back to the car, my belongings were either stashed in what I loosely referred to as "my bedroom," actually the guest room, or piled high in the laundry room. In the kitchen, I opened the fridge and grabbed a Coke. After the three-hour drive, I was too exhausted to make myself anything to eat and plopped my ass down onto the couch, turned on the TV, kicked off my Vans, and peeled back the tab on the can. This was exactly what I needed.

At my fraternity, solitude was hard to come by. The Sigma Nu house was one of the top fraternities at UCLA, and there were always people hanging out. Brotherhood, beer, and girls were plentiful, whereas privacy and a good parking spot were scarcities. There was a television in the house, but the only thing that was ever on was sports. In all my time at school, I couldn't remember ever once watching TV by myself. Of course, between school, studying, and working most weekends, I didn't have much time for it anyway. Yet, at home, alone, remote in hand, I felt like a god. I was happily surfing the channels when the phone rang.

I let it ring several times before making a halfhearted move to answer it. I knew it wasn't for me and I didn't feel like taking a message. I wished they would just hang up, but the ringing persisted, and I felt obligated to answer it. I made my way reluctantly to the kitchen desk.

"Hello?"

"Is Kent there?" a woman's voice asked.

I was rendered momentarily speechless upon hearing my name. After all, I was positive no one had this number.

"This is he," I answered at length.

"Hi Kent, this is Opal Milton," came the voice.

I was stunned. I didn't know what to say. I finally replied as casually as possible, "Well . . . this is a surprise. Uh . . . how are you?"

"I'm good," she said. "Everything's fine, like it's supposed to be."

Still her voice had a nervous high pitch to it.

"How did you know I would be here?" I said. "I mean, how'd you get this number?"

"I didn't know if you would be there, but it wasn't hard finding the number. There aren't too many Bernie Hildebrandts in the directory. You do know your stepfather is listed, right?"

"Uh . . . no, I didn't."

"Deciding to call you was harder, especially after all this time," she went on. "I needed to talk to you."

"It's been, what, over five years?"

"Yes, it's been a while. But you've been on my mind lately, and I thought I would take a chance."

"That's nice. So, thoughts of me still plague you," I said, with a hint of a laugh, trying to instill some humor into the conversation.

"They do, as a matter of fact," she said, deflecting my efforts at joking. Then she quickly changed the subject. "Tell me, what have you been doing all this time?"

Realizing I was being too cavalier, I dropped my defensiveness. Besides, she must have called for a reason.

"Where should I start? Right now, I'm a senior at UCLA, with a quarter to go, graduating early. Then, with any luck, a good law school next." Saying it aloud impressed even me, and it crossed my mind that it would be nice to throw my successes in her mother's face.

"UCLA and law school! My, that's impressive," she said. "How wonderful for you."

"Well, I haven't heard back from any of the schools I applied to yet, but hopefully soon. And you?"

"I've been in school too, but decided to take a year off."

"Then you're back in the States?"

"Actually, I'm back in Tustin, living with Mom and Dad in the old house."

"Wait, I'm confused. When did you get back?" I asked.

"Oh, I don't know exactly, maybe four years ago."

"What . . . and you waited until now to call me?"

"I couldn't. That's one of the reasons I'm calling you now. Is there any way we could get together and talk?"

"Absolutely," I responded without hesitation. "But what do you mean you couldn't?"

"I'd rather talk to you about it in person, if you don't mind. Do you have time this weekend?"

"Tomorrow's good for me," I replied, anxious to find out the whole story.

"Really?" She sounded surprised.

"Yes, really," I said sarcastically. "You said you're back at your old house? How about I pick you up at . . ."

"No, no," she interrupted me. "It would be best if I came to you. How's ten o'clock tomorrow morning?"

I gave her the address and directions.

"I'm really looking forward to seeing you," I said.

"Me too," and then she added more softly, "You know, I've never stopped caring about you."

"Tomorrow, then," I said.

"Good night," she said and hung up.

I WASN'T SURE what had just happened. My first love had called me. I quickly replayed every word of our conversation in my head, trying to make sense of it. She said I had been on her mind and that she had never stopped caring for me. What did that mean, especially after so many years? And she had moved back over four years ago and couldn't call me? It didn't make any sense.

I did my laundry in an attempt to stop obsessing. But thoughts of her kept filtering through. I became increasingly agitated, turning over all of the various possibilities in my mind. She did say she needed to talk to me—needed—not wanted. That could be good. Maybe. The more I speculated, the more I became tangled in knots. The pieces didn't fit.

There was only one thing I was sure of: I would get very little sleep that night.

Sleep is overrated. Nightmares can expose your insecurities . . .

Twenty-five

Whenever I'm consumed with something important, I can't sleep. And, true to form, all that night, I tossed and turned, thinking of her, replaying each word a dozen times over. My thoughts of graduation, law school, and even the current girlfriend had all evaporated. I knew they really hadn't vanished but undoubtedly were buried in some deep recess as an afterthought. I would have to thank Opal for yet another sleepless night.

Judging from our conversation, she was the same vivacious and mysterious Opal I remembered. I wondered what she looked like now. Did she still have her beautiful long blonde hair, or had she cut it short, maybe even dyed it some freakish color? Had she put on weight? It was hard to imagine her being fat. She had always been diet and health-conscious, long before those things became popular. In truth, I didn't care if she had gained a few pounds. For me, it had always been about her heart. Oh, don't misunderstand me, there was always a powerful attraction, but what I loved most about her was us. When I was with her, I even liked myself.

Having showered, shaved, and prepped myself hours earlier, I now sat in the living room watching the old Regulator wood wall clock, making a game out of it. I scrutinized the pendulum as it swung from side to side, each arc marking the passage of a second. I would glance at the clock's minute hand, look away, and then back again, to see if I could catch the hand as it pushed forward. Not once did I actually witness its progress. Somehow it moved only when I wasn't looking. Finally, bored with that game, I picked up a book lying on the end table—one of my mother's trashy romance novels. I did a cursory leaf-through, which kept me busy for all of ten seconds, then tossed it back onto the table, almost knocking over my half-empty cup of coffee.

When the big hand finally reached twelve and the chimes rang out announcing ten o'clock, I found myself counting each dong. I wondered if everyone counted the number of chimes even when they already knew what time it was. Still, it was a relief knowing it wouldn't be much longer.

I was taken almost by surprise when I heard the slam of a car door. My pulse quickened, and I took a deep breath. Could it be her? I went to the window to take a look. Walking around a tan-colored car was a dazzling young woman. Her thick blonde hair bounced as she came up the walk. She was more striking than I remembered, her fair skin setting off her radiant light blue eyes. Even from a distance, I could see her face was flawless. She wore a white cashmere sweater and jeans that tastefully showed off her exquisite figure. She was fit and curvy in all the right places. I took a step back, not only because I didn't want her to see me but also to catch my breath. After all this time, she still left me breathless.

There came a light tap on the front door. I waited a few seconds before opening it, so as not to appear overeager. Upon opening the door, I stepped forward and gave her a hug. She returned my embrace. It was more than just a polite courtesy hug, it felt more like a rediscovering-a-long-lost-friend-I'll-never-let-you-go-again-type hug.

"How are you?" I asked as I released her. I noticed that she let her hand linger on my arm a little longer than usual. "Well, come on in," I said, beckoning.

"You look great," she said, ignoring my initial question.

"Thanks. My hair's a little shorter and not as blond anymore . . . ," I said, then paused. "But you, you're even more beautiful than the last time I saw you."

"You're sweet. Thank you," she said with a smile.

Taking her hand, I led her down the hall and into the living room.

"Can I get you something to drink?" I asked, letting go of her hand and pointing to the couch. "Please have a seat."

"Nothing. Thank you," she said as she sat down.

"I hope you didn't have any trouble finding the house?" I asked, suddenly conscious that I was doing all the talking.

"No, your directions were perfect."

I could tell she was nervous by her clipped responses and by the perspiration I had noticed when I took her hand.

"I thought we could take a drive to the beach and grab a bite there," I said heartily. "What do you think?"

"Good idea," she said. "But first there are some things I need to tell you."

"Sure," I said, nodding. I sat down next to her, leaned back, and waited for her to speak. Having no particular expectations, I was intrigued by her fidgety and apprehensive manner.

She scooted to the edge of the couch.

"I told you we've been back for four years now. . . ." She paused and then leaned forward, resting her elbows on her knees, hands clasped together under her chin.

"Let me start from the beginning," she continued. "We didn't move to London as I was told. Instead we went to Texas. I only found out once we were inside the Dallas/Fort Worth terminal. I thought we were going to change planes, but then Mom took me aside and said, 'This is your new home and you need to accept it,' while Dad picked up the bags."

"Whoa. . . . So why the big cover-up?" I asked, intrigued.

"Remember, we were so much in love? They were afraid I'd try to contact you if I knew where we were going. London is one thing, Dallas is another. It's not exactly right around the corner but a lot closer than Europe. They thought if you found out I was in Texas, you would come for me somehow, and I would have wanted you to."

"They were right. I would have."

"And that's why I didn't call or write. I was heartbroken when we left, but after thinking about it, I understood that it was best the way it ended. I believed we were in Dallas for good and had to start my new life there, although I didn't talk to Mom for a month, and I cried for the first six. I missed you so much."

Leaning forward I could see tears form in her eyes. I grabbed her hands, noticing their warmth and softness, no longer exhibiting any sign of nervousness. The scent of strawberries drifted from her hair.

God, I've always loved the way she smells, I thought.

"Then we moved back here about 14 months later, to the same house. I finished my senior year at Tustin High. You had already graduated."

"Why didn't you call me then?" I asked, bewildered.

"I couldn't."

"I know. You said that last night, but . . ."

"I couldn't because I promised my parents. They gave me a choice: Stay in Dallas or move back here, but either way, I had to promise not to have any contact with you as long as I lived under their roof. I thought at least I could finish out school with some of my old friends. But mostly, I knew I would be that much closer to you, even if you didn't know it."

"If it were me, I would have called anyway," I said, feeling betrayed. "I mean, once you were back here, it's not like your parents could have just packed up and moved again."

"Yes, I know you would have, but you know me. When I give my word, I keep it. You wouldn't believe how many times I went into a store or walked home from school, hoping I would accidentally run into you. That way I could keep my promise, yet still see you."

Above all things, she was honest and true. I wanted to be mad at her, but I couldn't.

"I tried calling you once, after first getting approval from my folks. It was right after I graduated. I spoke with your brother. He said you were off at UCLA doing great; you were in a fraternity, and even had a girlfriend. I made him swear not to tell you I called."

"Great, the only time my big-mouth brother ever kept his mouth shut, and it had to be about you." Frustrated, I blurted, "I can't believe this."

"Please don't blame him. I asked him not to—it's my fault. I didn't want to force it. The timing wasn't right, and you already had a girlfriend. I just wanted you to be happy. That's all I ever wanted. It doesn't mean I stopped thinking about you, because I never have."

Wow, this was a lot to take in. I wanted to tell her that after she left I was a mess. I moped around, barely talked, and cried, especially at night when no one was around. I wanted to tell her I had never stopped thinking about her either.

Instead, I barked back, "Yes, I had a girlfriend then, and many after her, too. But none of them, not a single one, ever compared to you, including the current one. I wish you would have given me a little more credit and let me make my own decision."

"I'm sorry, you're probably right. That's why this is even harder to say." She let go of my hand, reached into her pocket and pulled out a diamond ring.

"I'm engaged," she said.

I felt like I had been sucker-punched in the back of the head. So, what was she doing here? What did she want from me? My blessing? No way in hell that would happen. She had led me on, giving me hope that there might be something between us, and now she was snuffing it out. I would have been better off had I not seen or heard from her at all.

Without revealing my inner turmoil, I said flatly, "I guess the timing is bad for both of us, yet again."

"Well, I'm not married yet," she snapped, not looking at me. "I had to see you and talk to you in person."

Now completely baffled, I asked, "So, what are you trying to say? Where am I in all of this?"

"All of this leads me back to you, today, and then . . ."

"Then what?"

"Then let's just see where today takes us."

There it was . . . another glimmer of hope. I couldn't figure it out, was she playing me? Though she did have a point. Maybe I could take this moment and see where it led. What if there was still something between us?

Ignoring my common sense, which dictated that I kick her out right then and there, I merely smiled, catching another faint whiff of strawberries as she flipped her hair off her shoulders.

"Okay," I said, "you're right. Let's go. We have today, and that's long enough to create a new memory or two."

I took her hand and led her out the door to my car. I had a plan. After finding her again after all this time, I wasn't about to let her go so quickly, at least not without a fight.

They say you should be careful for what you wish for.

Twenty-six

The Balboa Peninsula is cool in December and the streets mostly abandoned, with the exception of the unheralded manual workers that arrive unnoticed and leave tired. Winter was not the tourist season, even in the sunniest of Southern Californian beach cities.

As we drove onto the peninsula, I hesitantly reached over and caressed the back of her hand, hoping she wouldn't reject my faint attempt for affection. I was pleased when she instinctively turned her hand over, took hold of mine and squeezed. We drove the remaining distance holding hands, letting go only when I needed to shift gears. It was comforting, her hand so small and delicate, mine larger and calloused, as it covered hers like the bark protecting a tree's soft living core. It felt inexplicably right.

All thoughts of her impending marriage were erased when I witnessed her taking off her engagement ring. She tried to do it inconspicuously, but I caught her when I glanced over during a right turn. The sight of the white band of skin where the ring had been gave me a surge of confidence. I was astonished at how rapidly old feelings for her came rushing back. Before, she used to be part of everything in my life. I loved the way she cared for every living thing, no matter how big or small. Her words were always tender, her heart trusting, yet so easily hurt. She spoke her mind, though she was sometimes overly concerned with what others might think or expect. From what I had seen so far, nothing about her had changed. If only we could recapture that magic. I had no idea how today would unfold, but I intended to make sure it was special, except this time, it was for me.

We parked on 15th Street, and I fed the parking meter with all the quarters I had to ward off the overzealous Newport Beach meter maids. I grabbed the extra coat from my trunk and draped it over her shoulders as we rounded the corner and started up the boardwalk. My plan was simple: a walk on the boardwalk, a little talk, food at one of the local spots, and then finally, a surprise. But knowing Opal, I shouldn't have expected things to go according to plan.

As if reading my mind, she stopped dead in her tracks, stepped sideways off the sidewalk onto the sand, and sat down on the curb.

"What are you doing?" I asked.

"I'm taking off my shoes, silly," she said, dangling one sneakered foot in the air. "I want to feel the sand between my toes. Come on, take 'em off."

I sat down next to her, rested my feet on the sand, and looked out at the ocean. Under my breath I said, "What's next, go running down the shore in our underwear yelling, 'I'm free, I'm free'?" and shook my head in disbelief.

"You're going to have to do better than that if you don't want me to hear you," she said. "And maybe, yes, just my bra and underwear. Don't forget, I know you, so watch it, Surfer Boy," she said, raising her eyebrows at me.

"Busted. Okay, so how's this?" I said, avoiding eye contact and removing my right shoe. "Oh yeah, I sure have missed you," I said, sarcastically, and intentionally more loudly than necessary.

Still sitting, I extended my arms outward like a theatre actor poised to take a bow. Then turning to her, I said without irony, "Okay, I have missed this—us."

"Not me," she joked, giving my left shoulder a hard shove just as I bent over, sending me toppling to the sand. I threw out my right arm and grabbed her hand, pulling her down with me. Lightly tackling her, I shouted, "Really, then why'd you call me?"

We wrestled like children, hurling sand everywhere. I rolled onto my back, allowing her to pin me, knowing with a flick of a leg I could easily have tossed her off. I had her right where I wanted, her chest heaving from exertion, her hands pinning my shoulders, as I lay perfectly relaxed, looking directly into her light velvety blue eyes.

"I give," I said.

"See, I can still take you," she panted.

She leaned forward and kissed me softly on the cheek, then quickly jumped to her feet.

"That's it? I let you win and all I get is one little peck?"

"Patience," she said—that one little word that had started it all.

And yet that single chaste kiss was more powerful than any I had experienced over the past five years. I knew my heart was in trouble.

We stood up, and I brushed the sand off us and took her hand, leading her down to the shore. We walked hand in hand, the sand at the water's edge cold beneath our feet, her smile carefree and full of joy.

We talked about the past, about her family, and even of how many children we each wanted, someday, though we never said with whom. She wanted three, I wanted two, so we settled on two and a half. She wasn't sure exactly how that would work, but I offered up, "If you had a girl, and she had your personality, then that would definitely make up the extra half." She agreed, and giggled, blushing.

When we got to the pier at 21st Street, we headed inland for a bite to eat. We put our shoes back on before crossing the street to order takeout from The Crab Cooker, a small local spot whose specialty was clam chowder and seafood. We both ordered the Manhattan clam chowder and ate it slowly as we walked the six blocks back to the car.

I was suddenly aware that time was flying by, and as soon as we reached the car, I hurried Opal into her seat and carefully shut the door. I sped the whole way, intent on reaching my destination before sunset.

I parked in front of a house near the tip of the Balboa Peninsula. From the street, all that was visible were two oversized, single-car garages divided by extra-large, double front doors, giving no hint of what lay beyond. We bypassed the massive front doors and went around to the side entrance. Taking her hand, I led her through the newly painted wood gate and down the hundred-and-fifty-foot walkway that led to the backyard.

Opal followed me in silence. Her half smile gave no clue to what she was thinking.

Behind the front façade lay a seven-thousand-square-foot mansion, a replica of an 18th-century French château. The pitched slate mansard roof and several thousand red bricks laid in the traditional Flemish bond pattern, with rectangle-cut stone quoins at the corners, enhanced its authenticity. From the arched doorways and domed copper entrance to the two classically round windows, called oculi, located just above the second-floor windows, the building was a piece of historic French aristocracy brought to life. The two-story home had been built in the 1970s by an owner who had spared no expense in precisely recreating the original. It reminded me of pictures I had seen of the Palace of Versailles, massive and imposing.

We went into the backyard, entering the expansive and immaculately manicured grounds. On the far side of the lawn, freshly trimmed ivy grew under six mature, sculpted ficus trees that stretched at least fifty feet down the property line, providing privacy from the neighbor. On our side, small white flowers were budding on the star juniper plants growing against several mature holly bushes extending to the back of the property. In the center of the yard was an immaculate, five-hundred-square-foot dichondra lawn. Pathways of pebbles surrounded it and wove their way through the grounds. Beyond the yard, the harbor waters provided a spectacular backdrop, with the owner's boat moored at the dock.

Off the house was a veranda made of the finest limestone slabs imported from Europe. Two elderly gentlemen sat out, drinking cocktails and watching the sailboats and yachts drift by. One sipped a bourbon and soda, the other a gin martini, straight up, no ice. Having spent many an evening with the two gentlemen, I had come to learn their drinks of choice. I could tell Opal was confused, wondering what we where doing here.

As we mounted the steps to the porch, I said to the bourbon drinker with the garish brown dye job, "Winslow, I would like you to meet Opal."

He stood up and extended his hand, saying, "The pleasure is mine. Yes, you are quite lovely."

Turning to me, he said, "You were right, she is very fetching." Winslow was in his early sixties and often used two-dollar words such as "fetching." He came from old money and saw the world very differently than I did, though he did love people and hated the thought of growing old. He constantly surrounded himself with young people, enjoying their company and conversation. And no one ever said a word about his hair, as dreadful as the dye job was.

I watched Opal closely as she blushed. *Twice in one day*, I thought, *I'm on a roll.*

"Opal, this is Don Smith," I said, turning to the martini drinker. Don, also in his sixties, was, in contrast to Winslow, very distinguished looking. With his silver hair, tanned skin, and striking light blue eyes, he was thought handsome by most of the women in their social circle.

"Nice to meet you, dear," Don said, also standing to shake her hand.

She gave a hint of a laugh. "Nice to meet both of you gentlemen," she said. "Kent didn't tell me where we were going."

"He's like that," Winslow said, "unpredictable and, at times, presumptuous. Not to mention modest."

"Why yes, he is," she responded enthusiastically.

A little too agreeable, I thought. *Yep, she's the same old Opal.*

"Winslow, be polite in front of the boy," Don interjected. "We're here to help him."

"Help him?" said Winslow. "From the looks of things, he's doing fine without us."

"Hush now, Winny," said Don. "You two should get along now and leave us old men alone."

"Speak for yourself, you old bastard," Winslow retorted. "I'm still young."

"Don's right," I said. "We should go before its gets too late."

We said our goodbyes, crossed the yard, and walked out onto the dock. The *Bon Vivant* was a sleek, 23-foot Italian day cruiser made completely of wood—teak and mahogany being the most prominent. I helped her onto the boat and cast off.

Opal was speechless. That alone was an accomplishment. And twice I had gotten her to blush. I knew others had tried, but I was the only one who had the power to embarrass her at will. Once we were free of the dock and waving goodbye, she finally asked, "Who are those men?"

"Winslow and Don," I said.

"I know that," she said, slapping me on the shoulder. "And where are you taking me?"

"We're going to watch the sunset. I thought it would be a great way to end the day. Then maybe I just might let you in on a secret or two."

I took control of the wheel outside the open-air cabin and pushed the throttle stick forward. She stood next to me, slipping her arm through mine and resting her head on my shoulder. I could feel her warm breath through my shirt as we began our cruise, motoring past several large mansions that lined the Back Bay.

"No, really, tell me, who are they?" she said softly.

"All right . . . if you must know," I said sarcastically.

"Stop that and tell me."

"Okaaay. . . . I met them the summer break of my freshman year at UCLA. I filled in for Scott. You remember Scott, right?"

"Yeah, your old neighbor friend," she said, looking up at me.

"Well, Winslow bought this boat from Scott's dad and then hired Scott to help maintain the grounds. You've seen how big the property is—there's always something to do. Anyway, Scott asked me to work for him one Saturday, and I haven't missed a Saturday since, except for today.

"So, you're standing next to Mr. Handyman. I cut the lawn, trim the trees and bushes, paint, do odd repair work, and anything else to keep the place looking flawless.

"Here, take the wheel. Keep it steady—go straight. I'll be back in a second."

I left her at the helm and went down into the cabin. I emerged carrying two plastic glasses, a bottle of Riesling, and a corkscrew.

"What are you doing?" she gasped. "How did you pull all this together?"

"I called Winslow last night and explained everything to him. He offered to help."

"You're amazing," she said as she watched a seagull fly overhead.

"Now, you talk about a big job," I went on, "Try varnishing this boat. I've done it a few times. The worst was replacing the boat's bilge pump system. That sucked. You wouldn't have believed the smell."

"What about the other man? Don, right?" she asked.

"Oh yeah . . . Don's his good friend," I responded. "They've been business partners for years. I think they first met serving in World War II. But Don's really the one who tells me what to do around the house. They're both great guys."

"Wow," she paused. "All right, I don't mean to change the subject," she hesitated again. "But, you have to tell me one of those secrets of yours."

"I'm coming around to one," I said, as I extracted the cork from the bottle and began pouring its liquid gold contents. I handed her a glass.

"Okay, you remember, I didn't exactly have the happiest childhood. Well, as it turns out, the man who I thought was my dad wasn't my dad at all."

"What?"

"Wes. Remember this?" I said, setting down my glass and putting her hand to the back of my head where I still carried the scar left by Wes's certainty stick. I let her take a quick feel and quickly moved around and took charge of the boat again.

"I remember," she said sadly.

"He was not my real dad!" I said louder than I meant to. "When I was seventeen, Danny told me that Wes was his father but not mine or Sissy's. I confronted Mom and she finally broke down and told me the truth. My biological dad left when I was a baby.

"If you want to know the truth, I felt betrayed by my whole family. Everyone knew it but me. Actually, I don't know which is worse: having an asshole for a father, or not having one at all."

"And why didn't anyone tell you before?" she asked.

"I swear, to this day, I don't know, and still no one will talk about it. At least now I know why Wes spent so much time with Danny while I was left out. It also helps explain, maybe a little, why he hit me for everything Danny did wrong. Truly, I thank God he's not my dad. Of course, the hardest part was I had no one to confide in. You had been gone for months, and that was when I missed you the most. I was alone."

"I'm so sorry. I wish I could have been there," she said, giving me a reassuring hug. "What about your biological father? Do you know where he is now?"

"According to Mom, he's dead. Murdered or something like that when I was three or four. She's never elaborated. Whenever I asked a question about him, she'd refuse to answer. It doesn't matter, though. I've got Winslow. We've gotten pretty close over the years. He has no family of his own, apart from Don, and with Grandpa Heil gone and I was down a father myself, we were an ideal match. He's the closest thing to a true father I've ever had."

"How lucky are you?" she said, and snuggled up to me once again. "It seems it's all worked out for the best, the way it was supposed to."

We navigated past the end of the jetty that marked the edge of the Newport harbor and the beginning of the open ocean. At the helm with Opal by my side, I was content. *Maybe it did all work out for the best*, I thought.

The cool moist ocean breeze lightly misted our faces as we forged directly into the onshore winds. The fine water vapor clung to our exposed skin and I marveled at her, the way the saltwater coalesced into individual water droplets, making her glow. The golden light of the late afternoon sun reflected rainbow colors in the droplets, giving her face an angelic appearance. As the sun was about to set, I cut the motor so we could take in the moment. Together, we watched as it touched the surface of the ocean and the clouds turned shades of orange, pink, and purple.

We stood hand in hand, eyes on the horizon, swaying in the gentle ocean current.

"Thank you," she said. "I know you did this for me. This is unbelievably special."

I said nothing, but heard a soft laugh and turned to see her smile. I knew I was falling for her. For several minutes, neither of us spoke as evening encroached on the day's light.

UNFORTUNATELY, THE DAY had slipped by, and I didn't have to look at my watch to know it was late. I longed for more time, but I knew she would have to be getting back. In any case, I intended to steal her away the next day, so keeping her out later tonight might only make that possibility more difficult.

I piloted us back to the dock, and we thanked Winslow and Don for the use of the boat and for their hospitality. I drove slowly home, not wanting it to end. We had held hands all day—in the car, on our walk, in the boat, and now again in the car. At each juncture, my longing to kiss her intensified. There had been several opportunities throughout the day, but

I was waiting for just the right moment. Actually, I had let several right moments pass. Nonetheless, I had my sights set on a goodnight kiss.

We reached home as the night's solid blackness took hold. I opened her car door.

"Here you go," I said.

"I have something to tell you," she said as she got out of the car. "Come closer."

I leaned down and she grabbed my face with both hands and kissed me. I was shocked, surprised, elated, but it ended almost as soon as it started. It was a quick, closed-mouth kiss, certainly an improvement from the peck on the cheek she had given me earlier, but I wanted more.

"It's okay to kiss me," she said. "I've been waiting patiently all afternoon."

Needing no further encouragement, I drew her close to me. I slowly and deliberately moved my lips to hers, staring at her pouting mouth in anticipation of what I had been yearning for all day. Our lips touched ever so lightly; hers were soft and full with excitement. Our lips parted and our tongues met, unhurriedly twining around each other. I took in her breath and exchanged my air for hers. It was as if our individual souls had melded. My desire for her grew stronger with each breath and my heartbeat quickened with pleasure.

After a few minutes, she pulled her lips away from mine. I moved my mouth down to her neck, tilting her head back, cradling and caressing it. She grew limp in my arms.

"I have to go," she whispered hesitantly, wilting further.

I moved to the other side of her neck, and she moaned with pleasure.

"Are you sure?" I asked, not stopping.

"Mmmm . . . yes . . . no . . . yes . . . now stop . . . otherwise, I'll have to stay."

"Stay, then," I replied without thinking. *Wait . . . I didn't mean that.* I wanted her, but not that way. I had to stop myself.

"You know I can't," she said.

"You're right. What about tomorrow? Can I see you?"

"Oh, yes . . . absolutely. But it has to be later. I need to clear up a few things in the morning."

I didn't ask her what those things might be.

"How about noon, then, back here?" I suggested.

"Noon would be great," she said. "I can't wait to see you."

We hugged and shared another long, sensual kiss before she finally drove off, waving all the way down the street. What a perfect day. When I had planned it the night before, I couldn't have imagined it going any better. Mostly, though, I was shaken by what I was feeling for her. Again.

I had one reservation: How was I going to top today?

Twenty-seven

I knocked on the door. After a moment, it slowly creaked open.

"What are you doing here?" Opal looked horrified. "I thought we were meeting at noon at your place."

She was still in her pajamas, light blue, dotted with gray and white cherubs.

"I know . . . I realize it's only nine o'clock, but I couldn't sleep, and I was thinking of you, and . . . I just had to bring you this." From behind my back I brought out a single white rose.

Whatever confused and anguished state she was experiencing instantly evaporated, replaced by a smile that stretched from ear to ear. She took the rose and jumped into my arms, hugging me fiercely.

"I've missed you, too," she whispered softly. "I thought about you all night long. Let me get dressed and meet you back at your house," she said, letting go of me. "I need to get out of here."

"Hey, there's no reason to change, Angel Girl," I said, admiring her pajamas. "What you got on is perfect. You look soooo, what? Heavenly."

"Shush . . . ," she said, as she patted my chest, at first reproachfully, then spreading her fingers and letting them linger. "Where we going anyway? What should I wear?"

"Something warm. We're going to the snow."

"No way!"

"Yes way," I said, pausing to take in her excitement. "How about skiing?"

"Great! Okay, okay. Go, go, go now, and I'll meet you at your place in twenty minutes."

She's trying to get rid of me. I didn't care. She was mine for another day.

I kissed her goodbye, and she shut the door. As I turned to leave I could hear her voice on the other side of the door but couldn't make out what she was saying. Impulsively, I peeked through the front window into the family room. She had her back to me, and as I watched she threw her left arm high in the air, lowered it, and then raised the right arm, still clutching the rose, and then lowered it. Her arms continued this seesaw motion, up and down, and then her bottom joined in, swaying from side to side. She was dancing, and singing a song to herself. I couldn't quite make out the words, but as I watched, I could believe she might have started to fall for me. As for me, it was already too late. I was in love with Opal.

* * * * * *

EXHAUSTED AFTER TWO consecutive nights with almost no sleep, I fought to stay alert for the hour and a half drive up to Big Bear. I was thankful that the mountain roads were clear of snow and the day relatively warm for this time of year—somewhere in the low forties. Opal dozed for most of the trip. Awakening from time to time, she would seek out my hand and give it a gentle squeeze before shutting her eyes again. I assumed she was feeling as physically and emotionally drained as I was. Even so, I was happy that she was comfortable enough to sleep in front of me, even letting out an occasional snort or two. But by the time we had rented our equipment in Running Springs, she was wide awake and hung on my every word the rest of the way.

We got to Snow Summit in record time, 109 minutes including the stop for rentals. I paid for the lift tickets, and we skied over to the shortest lift line, both of us dying to get onto the slopes. Once ensconced in the chair lift, our skis dangling thirty feet above the snow-covered ground, I put my hand on her thigh.

"Hey, sweetie, this morning at your house, I got the feeling you were trying to get rid of me."

"I was," she said, looking away.

"Well, why?"

"I knew you were going to say something. . . . Okay, it's just that Mom and Dad were at church and I thought they might be back at any moment. I didn't want them to catch me on the front porch in my pajamas, holding a rose . . . and you, standing there. It would have been . . . awkward."

"Understandable. Then, how'd it go last night when you got home?"

"Fine. Oh, you mean apart from all the screaming and yelling."

"What?"

"Got you," she said, nudging my arm with her shoulder. "Yeah, Mom asked me a bunch of questions, like, where were you? Who were you with? That sort of thing."

"And?"

"I told her I was out with a friend. She let it go, and that was the end of it. Then I went to my room and thought, it's none of her business anyway."

"Then why the big hurry this morning if that's the case?"

"Because of you, silly boy. I wanted to be with you today and I didn't want any hassles from them."

"Everything's good, then?" I asked, not really wanting to know.

"Great, except for one problem."

"Yeah?" I asked nervously.

"For some reason, I haven't been sleeping well lately. It might have something to do with the company I've been keeping."

"Now just hold on a second, Miss Car Bedhead who slept the entire drive up here. Did you know you snort in your sleep?"

"I do not," she protested.

"Oh, yes, you do. Every once in a while you'll let out a small shallow snore followed by a snort. It's actually quite amusing but definitely a snore and then a snort."

"I do not. And if I did, it's all your fault. I've been thinking about you way too much and it's obviously affected my sleep patterns. That's my story and I'm sticking to it." She crossed her arms and raised her chin.

"Now let me get this straight," I said. "You can't sleep because you're thinking about me. And because you're so tired from the lack of sleep, you snort? Sounds about right to me. Yep, it's entirely my fault."

"Shush, you. And what's wrong with my hair?"

"Nothing, you look great. Watch out."

The drop-off point was coming up quickly. We hopped out of the chair and skied over to the top of the runs. On the crest were several routes down. I selected what looked like the easiest one. Peering over the edge, I took a moment to adjust my jacket and gloves. I leaned in close to Opal so only she could hear me.

"Hey," I said, "I watched you sing and dance your way through the house this morning. You were, oh . . . very sexy. Great hip action, too." Before she could react, I pushed off over the ledge, laughing.

As I skied down the hill, chuckling, I spotted out of the corner of my eye a red-faced, blue blur, and it was gaining on me. Before I knew it, I was bouncing off a small hill and had fallen onto my back, spinning around like an upturned turtle, carrying a passenger along for the ride. We slid to a stop in the middle of the run—one of my skis had popped off and come to rest some thirty yards away, while the other remained firmly attached to my boot. Opal lay on top of me, red-cheeked and breathless.

"You saw me?" she panted.

I laughed even harder.

"You mean this?" I said, extending my right arm over my head and bringing it down while simultaneously extending my left arm on the icy ground mimicking her moves from that morning.

"Stop it," she said, laughing now as well. She gently rested her head on my chest, and hugged as much of me as she could get her arms around, smiling with embarrassment. I threw my arms around her, and we held each other.

"Nice body slam," someone shouted as he skied past.

"He's right, good takedown," I said. "You okay?" I asked as I dropped my arms to the ground.

"I'm fine," she said. "Besides, as long as I end up on top, how could I get hurt? How about you?"

"I'm always all right when you're around."

She inched her way up my body until she was facing me and kissed me. In two days, my world had been turned upside down. Was it too soon to tell her what I felt? To tell her that I had never stopped loving her? That I was madly in love with her all over again? Maybe I should wait? She had crushed me before. She was the only woman who had ever broken my heart. I kept on kissing her and said nothing.

"Hey, you two, get a room," a teenager bellowed as she skied by.

"Let's get skiing," I said. "I'll bet you lunch I can beat you to the bottom."

We stood up, and I located my other ski further down the hill. Luckily it had become entangled in one of the emerging pine saplings growing on the trail's edge. By the time I clicked my boot back into the ski, she was off. Way down the hill, I could see her speeding away.

PAYING FOR LUNCH at the Bear Bottom Lodge could have been more humiliating. Not because she beat me, but due to the several spectacular tumbles I'd had on the way down. Thank God she had been too far ahead of me to witness any of them.

By the time I got to the bottom, she had been waiting for me a good five minutes.

We spent the rest of the day playing our parts as a newfound couple. We held hands, kissed, exchanged longing glances—to all appearances, happy young lovers.

As we waited in line with our lunch trays, an elderly lady commented to her husband, "Look, dear, they remind me of us. They just look like they belong together."

Yet we never gave voice to our feelings. I hoped and prayed that she could tell how I felt by my actions and that I was right in assuming she felt the same way.

* * * * * *

NORMALLY, AFTER A day of skiing, I would make a beeline for the highway to try to beat the traffic home. Today was different. I didn't care if there was traffic or not. I treasured every minute with her. There were surprisingly few cars as we drove down the mountainside watching the sun set. But, in keeping with everything else that had happened over the past few days, it couldn't have been better.

When I looked over at her, I could see she was worn out. She leaned back in her seat, eyes open, but glazed over, staring at me. She had pulled down the top of her ski suit, revealing a white turtleneck with three narrow green stripes across the chest. I took in the view, admiring how the sweater clung tightly to her breasts while accentuating her small waist. She had blossomed into a beautiful woman. More importantly, today I had rediscovered her heart, as pure as the day I first met her. I felt blessed to have her back in my life.

"What are you thinking?" she asked, rousing me out of my reverie.

"You."

"And?"

"It's as if nothing has changed between us. Regardless of how much time has passed, we're still the same. It just feels right."

"I was thinking the same thing," she said. "I feel comfortable with you. Like I can tell you anything."

"You can. Anything. I'm here for you, always."

She was silent. She smiled broadly, and then with a hint of a giggle, brought her hand up, covering her mouth. Words were not needed. Contented, I drove on.

* * * * * *

"CAN YOU STAY a while?" I asked as we pulled up to my house.

"I should go," she said.

My head drooped and my shoulders dropped in disappointment.

"But I think I'll stay," she added quickly. "Besides, I'm starving. What's for dinner?"

With renewed excitement, I led her into the house. Part of me wanted to make mad passionate love to her right then and there. She had stirred the innermost part of me. But how could I make love to her when she was with another man?

There was so much turmoil in her life, I didn't want sex to become an issue. As much as I wanted her physically, it was her heart I craved most. Until she ended her engagement, I wouldn't truly have all of her.

We kissed for several minutes on the family room couch before she said she wanted to take a shower. She complained that her clothes "smelled of the day," so I gave her my lone Brooks Brothers white button-down shirt, a pair of white socks, and pajama bottoms to change into. While she showered, I collected the ingredients for chili, one of only three things I knew how to cook—hamburgers and steak being the other two—when I didn't undercook or burn them beyond recognition. I left the beans to simmer and jumped into my parents' shower down the hallway from where Opal was.

When I got back to the kitchen, Opal was stirring the chili, looking sexy in the shirt that came down to her knees, sleeves rolled up, and not wearing the pajama bottoms I'd given her. I came up behind her, put my arms around her and gently kissed her on the neck. She kept stirring. She seemed so serious.

"Are you okay?" I asked, still holding her, then moved around to see her face.

"I'm just happy," she said, a tear trickling down her cheek.

"Then why the sad eyes?"

"Not sad. You know me, they're tears of wonder. Let me enjoy this moment, this feeling of you, okay?" I started to let go of her. "No, please, don't let go. Just be here with me. Keep holding on."

We stood before the stove, the burners blazing, watching the chili, swaying in silence. She stirred the pot, and I held her, not wanting anything more than this. If I were ever to define love, it would be that moment.

A couple of hours later, we had finished eating and washed and put away the dishes. We sat on the floor in front of the fireplace, my back against the couch, she between my legs, her head resting on my chest, my arms wrapped around her shoulders. As the fire roared, its light flickered and bounced off of her face and neck. I was finding her beauty increasingly difficult to resist. My oversized shirt disguised her exquisite figure, and yet she was somehow all the more enticing because of it. Earlier, I had noticed that she was braless and caught glimpses of her white cotton underwear when she turned too quickly. But again I reminded myself that we had to be a couple before we could sleep together. There couldn't be any fiancé or girlfriend in the picture. I knew what was right, or did I?

We talked, kissed, and hugged for hours, until she closed her eyes, exhausted. I picked her up, gently laid her on the couch, and covered her with a blanket. She snuggled up to a throw cushion and immediately drifted off.

"Opal, I love you," I whispered to her sleeping form and kissed her on the forehead.

I watched her for an hour, but then I knew I had to wake her. She couldn't spend the night. I stroked her hair to awaken her gently.

"Listen, sweetie," I whispered, "It's late. You have to go."

"Oh Kent, hon," she mumbled, still not awake, "No, I'm not going anywhere."

"Are you sure?"

She sat up.

"What time is it?"

"Almost two thirty."

"Wow," she said, some alarm creeping into her voice. "I do have to go."

Her head dropped back onto the cushions.

"Oooh, I want to stay," she said plaintively.

"There's always tomorrow. I mean, later today," I joked.

"All right," she said groggily, shrugging her shoulders and frowning.

I helped her up and sent her down the hallway to change. She walked slowly, one sock pulled up over her calf, the other dangling around her ankle, most of it dragging behind her. The shirt was wrinkled and had slipped off of her right shoulder while the sleeves now hung past her fingertips, flapping emptily as she walked. Her hair was disheveled and was everywhere except where it should have been. She looked like she had sex-hair—which is one degree worse than the repudiated bedhead look.

Yes . . . she is achingly beautiful, I thought.

Five minutes later she came back, dressed in her own clothes, hair neatly coiffed but with the frown still in place.

"You okay to drive?" I asked.

"It's only a few miles. I'll be fine."

"Then why the long face?"

"I don't want this to end."

"Nothing's ending. You're going home to sleep, that's all. I'm here for you." My reassurance had no effect. I sensed she had something to tell me, but that she was having trouble finding the words.

"Thank you for today," was all she said.

"You're very welcome. Listen, you're tired. Can you come back tomorrow, so we can spend the whole day together?"

"All right," she replied, but she looked sad.

I walked her to her car and gave her a kiss goodbye. As she drove off, I felt uneasy. Everything had been good up until the moment she had to leave. What had she meant when she said, "I don't want this to end"? Too drained to think, I went to bed.

I lay there for an hour, tossing and turning. At four o'clock, I got up, went to the family room, and sat in front of the television, where I finally fell asleep.

Echoes of the past touched me that day.

Twenty-eight

The phone rang.

I rolled off the couch and stumbled over to it. The TV was still on.

"Hello," I said hoarsely.

"Good morning, hon," said Opal.

"It's nice to hear your voice first thing in the morning," I said, perking up immediately. "I could get used to this," confessing a truth, still half-asleep.

"Aren't you sweet."

"Why, yes, I am."

"Well, it's time to get up, sleepyhead. We need to talk. I'll be over in about twenty minutes."

"What time is it?" I asked.

"Eight thirty. You need to get ready for me, so get up."

When someone tells you, "We need to talk," it's never good news.

"I'm getting up," I said. "See you in a few minutes."

"Bye, hon," she said sweetly before hanging up.

I dashed out of the family room, took a quick shower, shaved, shook out a splash of cologne and was, I thought, all set. But feeling a breeze on my skin, I realized I had forgotten one thing—pants. I slipped on a pair of jeans that didn't come close to matching my brown striped Hang Ten T-shirt, and then quickly made my way to the kitchen to make a pot of coffee. I added the Folgers to the coffee maker, poured in the water, closed the lid, and pressed the button, but before I could even sit down, the doorbell rang.

My heart skipped a beat. I fought back my insecurities, asking myself, how could this be bad? We had just spent two wonderful days together. I put on a smile. All was well.

I opened the door with a big fake smile. She kissed me on the cheek, and walked past me into the house.

"Are you coming?" she asked as she headed for the kitchen.

"I've been doing a lot of thinking," she continued, "and we've talked a lot over the past few days. But, there's one subject we've both avoided."

She pulled out a chair and sat down at the kitchen table. Positioning a chair directly in front of her, I sat down.

Here it comes, I thought, the *"It's not you, it's me" speech.*

"You know I'm engaged, right?" she said, looking straight into my eyes. "How do you feel about that?"

I took her left hand, acutely nervous about the direction the conversation was taking.

"I don't like it," I said. "When are you supposed to get married anyway?"

"Two weeks from last Saturday."

"Two weeks! Wait . . . that's less than two weeks . . . what—twelve days? No, I don't think so. I can't let that happen."

"But, what about your girlfriend?" she asked, turning it back onto me.

"What about her?!" I said aggressively, voice rising. "Friday night, right after we spoke, I decided—she's gone."

"Just like that," she said, snapping her fingers. "Why?"

"Because of you," I said, regaining my composure. "Since we first talked, I haven't thought of anything else. Saturday confirmed with every fiber of my being that we belong together. And then yesterday, oh yesterday . . . all I wanted to do was hold you."

Leaning in, I put two fingers on her lower lip and gently traced the outline of her mouth, "And kiss those beautiful lips of yours. Every waking moment, every dream I've ever had, it's been you, always you, and no one else. I'm in love with you."

Her smile lit up her face, filling her eyes with joy.

"I was hoping you felt that way, because I love you, too. I've never stopped loving you."

We kissed and held each other for several minutes.

"So what are we going to do?" she said at last.

"Isn't it obvious?" I said. "I'll break up with Diana, and you've got to call off the wedding."

"Oh my god," she said, shakily. "This is going to be a mess. Everyone's furious with me already. Steven and my mom want to know where I've been the last couple of days."

She put her hands to her mouth.

"Invitations were sent out two months ago," she went on, her agitation mounting, face flushed. "We have more than two hundred people coming. The church, the reception room, it'll all have to be canceled. God. . . . We have family flying in, too. Mom's going to kill me."

"But do you love him?" I asked.

"Yes . . . but no. At least, not like this," she said, grasping my hand. "What we share is more intense, yet effortless. Everything comes so naturally with you. That's what Steven and I are missing. With him, things are more . . . contrived. There isn't that overwhelming emotional pull like I have with you. I do love him, but it's just different."

"So what do you want? You can't have both of us."

"I want to be with you," she said emphatically.

"You sure? Maybe you're getting cold feet about the wedding," I paused. "Is that why you called in the first place?"

She let go of my hand.

"No! I had other reasons." She paused, calming herself. "Listen, Steven and I, we make a good couple, but, like I was trying to say, we lack the deep, powerful passion that makes a relationship great and not just good. Sure, I know he loves me dearly. And everyone likes him. He'll probably be a good family man, and money wouldn't be an issue. But, the love . . . oh, I don't know. So I had to ask myself, 'Is this man really my soul mate?' Well, it may have taken me some time, but I finally figured it out. I called you because I needed to know if what we shared was real, or just some naïve notion of our youth."

"Yeah . . . tell me," I said.

"You already know. It's as real today as it was five years ago. And I'm not just getting cold feet."

"Then why did you take so long to call me? Talk about waiting 'til the last minute."

"Oh. . . . That. . . ." She stopped and rubbed her face with her hands, then brushed her hair off her shoulders.

"All right. . . . Last Thursday I had dinner with Mom, just the two of us. We started talking about Steven and the other guys I've dated over the years. I guess she wanted to clear her conscience or something. Anyway, when it came to you, she revealed how she'd had a hand in ending our relationship and how it was the best thing she had ever done for me."

"And how exactly did she do that?" I asked, feeling the stirrings of the old loathing for her mother.

"The morning of the prom she told me we would be moving shortly after school ended. Yeah, I know I used the lame excuse of another guy. That was her idea. She said it would be best to cut it off as soon as possible. That way you wouldn't be as hurt later on. Anyway, the truth is, she had been lying to me all along. Dad was offered a job in London, but he turned it down. Mom took advantage of that to trick me into breaking up with you and to perpetuate the lie. As long as you were out of the picture, the date of the move kept getting pushed back. Sure enough, there never was any moving date. Then, when we got back together, it hit Mom even harder. About that time, Dad was offered another opportunity, a one-year training assignment in Dallas, which worked out perfectly for Mom. She said the real reason we left was because of you. She couldn't handle our obsession with each other. It was forever Kent, Kent, Kent. I was never home, and when I was, I was on the phone with you. The whole thing was too much for her and the whole family, though I think it was just her. She was afraid we'd do something stupid like get married right after graduation or maybe I'd get pregnant. So Dad took the job. She said the whole family needed the change."

"Huh, your dad transferred because of me? Hmmm. . . . I wonder how they're going to take the news that we're back together and the wedding is off."

"I don't want to think about that right now," she said, leaning against my chest. "Can you just kiss me?"

We kissed as if we were teenagers again. Our lips locked in raw passion while exchanging whispers of "I love you." Our hearts beat as one. I wanted to make love to her. It would have been right. But I knew I wouldn't.

"We need to go for a walk and cool down a bit," I offered. With a word she could have persuaded me otherwise. I hugged her tightly to prove my desire for her.

As if reading my mind, she said, "You're right, we can wait. We have a lifetime to make love."

When I stood up the bulge in my jeans was clearly visible. I pulled my shirt down to cover it.

"Whatcha got there, hon?" she asked, as she rearranged her own clothing.

"You'll find out soon enough," I said.

"Shush now. . . . Hey, did you know I love you?"

I recognized our special saying from many worlds ago.

"Why, yes, I do! But I love you more." I gave the customary response.

"Only for today, Kent, because tomorrow, I'll love you even more."

We held each other tightly. As I gazed into her eyes, I felt the love. She was smiling, seeming almost relieved. Not wanting to risk breaking the mood, I decided that the secret I had kept for all these years and now wanted to reveal would stay locked away, at least for today. I trusted that we had a lifetime to share and there would come a better time and place. The fact that it was I who had orchestrated that hoax phone call from Sissy wouldn't make any difference now. My accomplice, Linda, was the one who had made the call saying I had been hospitalized. My improvisational skills had rescued what could have been a disastrous situation. Though initially all I wanted to know was, did she still care about me? It's amazing what a broken heart can make a person do. But after all, it had worked. I'd gotten her back, at least for a while. Another time.

"It's going to be okay," I murmured. "We'll be together soon . . . forever."

I took her hand and we walked out the front door.

* * * * * *

I HAD ALWAYS enjoyed our walks—having the one I loved next to me, holding her hand, and feeling great about life. The smells of nature, the color of the sky, the bird songs, and the occasional wind chimes all seemed more intense, brighter, and had a greater meaning when I was with her. We walked for about an hour and discussed inconsequential things, just enjoying each other's company, until we were two blocks from home.

"I'm a little scared about what's going to happen," she said. "Aren't you?"

"No, I'm not," I said, lying, and then paused. "Well, let's talk about it and make a plan. Then it won't be so scary."

"Okay, but only if you make me a promise first."

"Promise you? Sure. What do you want me to promise? That I'll break up with Diana?"

"That's part of it," she said. "But mostly, I want you to promise that you will always love me."

"I promise, I will love you always," I said as I kept walking, looking around, believing she was only half serious.

"And?"

"I promise I will break up with my girlfriend," I said in a low, conspiratorial voice for comic effect. "I'm telling you right here, right now, I'll break it off tomorrow. What about you?"

She stopped me and looked me straight in the eye.

"I promise I will always love you. Oh, yeah . . . and that whole calling off the wedding thing, too."

"Then it's a plan, right?"

"Yes, absolutely," she said, now completely focused.

"Wait a second," I said, thinking a moment. "I do have one stipulation. Since you're obviously in a more difficult situation, I need you to call me as soon as you've broken it off with him, and not before. But, if you like, I would be happy to break the news to your parents. As a matter of fact, please let me tell your mom."

"No, I think I'd better handle them," she said. "But that's a promise, you silly boy."

We spent the rest of the day joking, laughing, kissing, and holding each other. We ate an early dinner so she could get home to talk with her parents. As we said goodbye, we reminded each other of our promises. We said "I love you," and, as I watched her drive off, I was happy.

Promises, promises.

Twenty-nine

I was so excited by the day's events that I wanted to do something I had never done before. I decided to buy a ring. The joy in my heart was so overwhelming I felt like I was going to explode. She was the one. I had always known it. Every thought and dream I had ever had about her was about to be realized. At last it was our time. No more having to worry about what her parents thought. Age was no longer a barrier. This time, love had won.

It was getting late, seven forty-five already, and the Orange Mall closed at nine o'clock. I would have to make it quick. I felt strongly that it had to be done that night or the magic would somehow slip away, and I didn't want anything to break the spell. I wanted this feeling to last for the rest of our lives.

I walked straight through the mall's sliding glass doors and headed directly to a small boutique, Rocco's Fine Jewelry. An Italian-looking gentleman, maybe in his early fifties, wearing an expensive pressed suit, stood behind the counter in a vaguely military stance.

"May I help you, sir?" he asked.

"Yes, I am looking for a ring, nothing too elaborate."

"And what is the occasion, if I may ask."

I didn't answer but scanned the display cases searching for the diamond engagement rings. Once in front of the case, I spotted a beauty.

"How much is that one?" I asked, pointing to what I thought was a reasonable-sized diamond in a gold setting.

He removed the ring from the case, put it on a mat on the counter, and read the tag.

"This one is $1,249," he said. "A wonderful diamond, a half carat with a good VS1 rating."

Knowing nothing about diamonds, I wasn't sure if that was a good deal or not. But the one thing I did know, I couldn't afford it.

"Oh, that's a little too much for me," I said, disappointed.

"Then approximately how much are you looking to spend?" he asked. "That will give me an idea how I can best serve you."

"What do you have in the $500 range?"

"Well, let's see what is in this case," he said, leading me to the obviously cheaper merchandise.

"What about something like this?" he asked, indicating to a ring with a barely visible speck of a diamond. The price was right, but it was small, puny. I couldn't give Opal something so tiny. Plus, the ring she already had, from him, was huge. It had to be something special, unique. Then it came to me.

"No, I'm looking for something completely different. It doesn't have to be a diamond. What about a gold band?"

The salesman came out from behind the counter and escorted me across the store to a case housing only bands.

"Is this what you have in mind?" he asked.

"Exactly. Can I see that one, please?" I said, pointing to the one I wanted.

He opened the back panel and removed it from the display. This time he laid the ring directly on the glass counter. I picked it up and gave it the once-over. It was a simple gold band. The width seemed right and the weight perfect. I glanced at the price.

"I'll take this one," I said without hesitation.

"Wonderful. Let me find you a box and . . ."

"Actually," I said, cutting him off, "can I have it engraved?"

"It shouldn't be a problem, sir."

"I want the engraving on the outside of the ring, and then to have the engraving filled in with white gold. Can you do that?"

"Yes, to the engraving—and that might be a little expensive," he said. "But I'm sorry, sir, the white gold fill won't be possible."

"No? Why not?" I asked, disheartened.

"The white gold would melt into the borders of the letters. It would be very difficult to read, if you could make out any letters at all."

"Are you sure?"

"Yes, sir, positive. I'm the master engraver here. Would you still like the band?"

"Yes, please. And I still want it engraved," I requested.

"You were lucky tonight," he said, picking up the ring to take a closer look. "I'm only here to fill in for an employee who had a family emergency. Come over to the register and let's see what we can do."

Before he turned to take me to the front of the store, I noticed he wasn't wearing a name tag.

"What's your name?" I asked.

"Lee Fontanella, sir."

"Nice to meet you. I'm Kent."

"The pleasure is mine. Now, what would you like on the band?"

I thought for a moment, and then suddenly came up with it.

"I want it to say: 'Tomorrow I'll love you even more.'"

He wrote it down and then started calculating the height and width of the letters to see if it would fit. After a few minutes he looked up.

"If I do the lettering in cursive writing, it will work. You made it by a couple of letters. It should take me about a week."

"Sold. How much?"

"Just a moment, sir," he said and left me for a back station.

After a few minutes he returned. "The ring is $339.00, and with the engraving, labor and tax, the total comes to $419.61."

I took out my checkbook and quickly determined that it would cost me almost every penny I had. But this was for the girl I was going to spend the rest of my life with. It was worth it.

"Who do I make the check out to?"

"Rocco's Fine Jewelry," said Lee Fontanella.

As I LEFT the store, I had a couple of things on my mind. First, how madly in love I was with Opal. But secondly, I had a nagging reminder that tomorrow I was going to hurt someone else's heart. Breaking up with Diana would be difficult, but it had to be done.

What a great day this had been. I couldn't wait to hear from Opal. I wanted to know every detail, every word that had been said. I wondered how Mother Milton would take the news. She would eventually learn to love me. After all, someday we would be family.

Maybe Opal would call tomorrow. Then we could start the rest of our lives together.

Part III

Promises of the heart are the hardest to keep.

Thirty

The call never came.

When I finally accepted that I had been passed over, forgotten, okay . . . dumped, I was devastated. Anyone who has experienced rejection knows how difficult it is to confront or accept. The hundred and one excuses I came up with included everything from total denial to blaming myself for everything. Avoidance worked well at first, but ultimately I ended up holding myself largely responsible for my own plight. Perhaps I had been too proud to make the short drive over to her parents' to fight for her. I've often wondered over the years how I could have allowed the distance of just six miles to keep us worlds apart. Or it may have been my own stubbornness in simply failing to pick up the phone to call her that sealed our fate. Being forced to face the reality that she didn't want me would have been more than I could endure. So, I let it slip away—not wanting to know "why" while lying to myself that I did all I could. Maybe those things I believed so strongly then are the reason the dreams have continued to this day.

Now I have to put an end to twenty-seven years of strange coincidences and countless dreams of her. Too many times in the past I have found myself at this juncture, and each time I have chosen to look the other way. I tell myself I will forget about it soon enough. And little by little, the feelings dissipate. The memories fade and then vanish—until the next time. The dreams are never truly gone; they hide away, much like the ring I bought that still languishes in my memory box, waiting.

But today is different. After all these years, I will set out to find her, to ask questions and get answers. To settle unresolved issues I have been, until now, too afraid to face. And most important, to put a stop to the dreams.

* * * * * *

I BEGIN MY search in the obvious place—on the Internet. I look up my own name first, which turns up some odd, random entries: a 10K run in which I finished 132nd (more than four years ago) and buried deep within a list of founding members of the El Toro Great Park. For Opal, after so many years, I don't have much to go on, other than her maiden name and an old street name—I don't even have the exact address. Chances are that neither is current. I find nothing on our high school website, or on any of the many reunion dot coms, nor in the online marriage and divorce records of the Orange County clerk's office. After hours of research, I have nothing. I conclude that she must be using her married name, and I have no idea what it is.

I drum my fingers on the desktop, unsure of what to do next. I lean back and look across the desk at the painting on the wall. I am convinced that it is a portrait of Opal, the likeness too uncanny to be mere coincidence.

"Opal, where are you?" I say aloud. She doesn't reply.

I think a moment longer.

"What if I checked your old home?" I say aloud again. "I'd love to see the old place."

I know it's unlikely her parents still live there, but there's always that possibility. Besides, it's not like I have a better idea. I turn off the computer and pick up a notepad and pen on my way out of the office.

I will have no problem finding the place, even after all this time. This will not, in fact, be the first time I've been by there in the intervening years. On those rare occasions I find myself in the area, I somehow always make the time to drive past the house. I stop at the local Yoshinoya for lunch and afterward drive the two miles out of my way to Opal's old neighborhood. During each of my drive-bys I have never seen anyone coming or going from the house. It's been at least six years since I was last in Tustin, and who knows how much has changed in that time.

If the Miltons aren't there, at least I can get the house number, which I'll need for research at the Hall of Records.

Tustin is a short twenty-mile drive from my home in Mission Viejo. Instead of taking the freeway, I opt for the easier but longer route via the back streets. I can use the extra drive time to come up with a few canned questions to ask her parents, just in case.

Obviously, the first thing out of my mouth can't be, "Where's Opal?"

I'll have to think of something a little smoother, like, "I was just in the neighborhood and thought I'd take a chance on seeing if you still lived here."

Then I could act all surprised and maybe give and get a hug or two. After that I could improvise and eventually find out where she lives and perhaps even get her phone number. I think it's a good plan.

Driving into Tustin and seeing those familiar streets, I feel the past rushing back. Though, somehow, it's a new feeling, one I didn't expect, and haven't experienced on any previous visit. The memories flood my senses, more vivid and real than ever before. Possibly because it's been so long since I was last here, or maybe the mere thought of seeing her again is making me a little nervous. Either way, it feels strange, even unnatural.

As I drive, each street I pass seems to evoke its own acute memory. At the corner of Irvine and Browning is the old Pac Bell building with big glass doors set back behind the brown brick entryway. Once, anchored to the brick wall, to the left of the doors, there was a pay phone from which I made countless calls to Opal, for a dime a pop. We could talk for hours but tried to limit ourselves to thirty minutes so as not to arouse Mother Milton's ire. But more often than not, the thirty-minute mark would come and go, both of us lost in our own world. The pay phone has since been removed, but holes remain in the bricks where it previously hung. The building itself has no sign or other identifying marks, so I don't even know if it is still in use.

Farther down, I turn right onto Holt Avenue. I cross a newly paved section of road. Off to the right, behind a new chain-link fence, is an overflow ditch, its concrete lining forming a "V" shape. Dead leaves, beer bottles, and a variety of other trash litter its dirt banks. Remnants of the old Irvine Company's train tracks run parallel to the ditch.

In what feels like another life, I once hung out there with a group of my friends before a party. Jenkins, one of my surf buddies, picked the spot because it was private and we could smoke a joint and drink the beers he had swiped from his parents. None of us had a car, so we were on foot and it seemed like a good idea at the time. We drank a few and smoked too much. We never did make it to the party.

After a couple more turns, I'm driving up her street. It feels like only yesterday I was last here. "Livingston" is spelled in white lettering on the street sign's green background. I slow down as I near the house. It beckons as if it has been waiting for me. I continue to have the powerful sensation of the past all around me. I make a U-turn and park across the street from her house, trying not to draw attention to myself. I'm like a detective in a dime-store crime novel, doing surveillance.

From my vantage point, the house is much smaller than I remember. It looks to be newly painted gray and in impeccable condition. Clearly someone lives there. There is a new front door, white, with an oval window cut out of it that makes the house look inviting. To the right of the door, a huge bay window dominates the façade where the large family room window used to be. The door and windows are the new, energy-efficient kind. The swing that I so often shared with Opal is gone, as is the entire front porch—replaced by plants.

The front walk is unchanged, bricks and concrete, ending in five steps to the front door. The lawn is meticulously cut, landscaped with a couple of weeping birch trees, some sago palms, and a stately old ficus.

I think about the endless conversations with Opal and her mother in that front room. The topics were mostly philosophical, but somehow it always came around to a discussion about God, or how the Lord had helped me overcome my circumstances. The Miltons were good Methodists. They attended church every Sunday and did penance for their every wrongdoing and even for the sins of others. I don't know if they were ever aware of the transgressions that Opal and I committed together.

As I sit reminiscing, the garage door groans open, and a new ivory Cadillac starts to back out. There is an older woman at the wheel. The car turns and comes to a stop next to mine. The passenger-side window slides down.

"Can I help you?" asks the driver.

I'm taken aback at being confronted, but then again, I'm glad to find anyone at home.

"I'm looking for the Miltons," I say.

Is this woman Mother Milton? I'm not sure.

Thirty-one

The woman has short, blondish gray hair and looks to be in her sixties. From what I can see, she is nicely dressed. She doesn't answer at first, and I can tell she is sizing me up, deciding whether to answer me.

"They moved several years ago," she finally responds. "I believe we're the fourth owners since then."

"Do you have any idea where they moved to?" I ask.

"I don't, but you can try Bob," she says, pointing past me to the house I'm parked in front of. "He and his family have been here over thirty years. Maybe he can help you."

"Thank you," I reply, genuinely grateful. "I will."

"You're welcome," she says. "And have a good day now."

Her window rolls up and she drives off.

Okay, so they don't live here anymore, that's a start, I think.

I get out of my car and walk up to Bob's front door.

I CAN HEAR the sound of the doorbell ringing inside. I wait a few seconds and impatiently push the bell again, then wait for what seems like an even longer time. I feel an ache in the pit of my stomach. The dull throb reminds me of the anxiety-induced pain brought on by my first experience of public speaking. He must not be home; I back away and start walking back to the car.

"Hello, can I help you?" A voice comes from behind me.

I turn to see a man, also in his early sixties, standing in the doorway. He is tan, distinctive looking, with gray hair sprinkled about his slightly balding forehead. He holds a cell phone to his ear.

"Are you Bob?" I ask from a few feet away.

"Yes," he says, and then, into the phone, "Can I call you back? I have someone here. Thanks."

He switches off the phone and slips it into the front pocket of his khaki shorts. He wears a Tommy Bahama short-sleeved Hawaiian shirt decorated with an array of bright red, orange, and yellow flowers. Brown sandals complete the comfortable Californian beach motif.

"Hi, my name is Kent Huffman," I say, returning to the door and extending my hand. "I'm an old friend of the Milton family. Your neighbor told me that you knew the Miltons?"

"Oh, yes, we used to be good friends," he says, his expression softening. "They moved—oh, it must be at least ten years ago now. But I know they still live in the area."

"I would love to get in touch with them," I say, wanting to reveal as little as possible. "Do you have any idea where they live? Any information you have, I would really appreciate."

"Not exactly. But I know they're close. I saw Stu and Fran last year at a neighbor's party. They mentioned they live nearby. You know Timmy owns his own construction business?"

"No, I didn't know that," I say. "It's been several years since I've heard from any of them."

He seems to think I'm looking for her brother Timmy, but I am not about to correct him. It feels odd referring to him as Timmy. I'm sure that, as an adult, he must go by Tim. Most likely, "Timmy" is reserved for family and old friends.

"Well, Timmy is quite successful—married, children, a big house, too. My understanding is his business is thriving, making quite a bit of money, at least that's what Stu said."

"That's great," I say politely. "I always knew he would do well. Is there anything else you can tell me? Maybe you have a number or an address where I can reach the Miltons?"

"I know Timmy lives in the area too. Sorry, that's about all I know. Why don't you try next door? The Westons have lived here even longer than we have. Maybe Mrs. Weston can give you more information."

"Thank you very much, Bob," I say, reaching out to shake his hand again. "I appreciate your time."

I start back down the walkway, but then stop. I have to ask. I turn back to him.

"Bob, wait. What do you know about Opal?"

"Opal—she was such a nice girl," he sighs. "She babysat our grandkids when they were young. She and her husband lived just around the corner from here." He points in the general direction. "Too bad she died so young."

Thirty-two

"What?!" I can't believe what he just said.

"You didn't know? Oh, I'm sorry to tell you."

"What happened?"

"I don't know the specifics, but it happened, I think, maybe three or four years ago."

Unable to breathe properly, all I want to do is leave. My knees start to feel weak, and my mind goes blank.

"Are you sure? Opal, their only daughter?"

"I believe so, son."

Fighting back the urge to call him a liar, I say, "Bob, I have to go now," even as I know I should stay and ask him more questions. Abruptly turning away, I practically run down the steps, not caring what he might think. At that moment, I don't care about anything.

Quickly driving away, I begin having breathing problems. I try to take a short breath . . . but nothing, then again . . .

still nothing. Another try; this time I am barely able to make my chest move. I pull the car over; afraid I may pass out from lack of oxygen. I lean over the steering wheel gasping for air. Finally I catch my breath. I sit in silence, in disbelief, wanting to cry, but my eyes remain dry.

"No, this isn't possible. He's wrong!" I yell out. Looking down, I notice my hands are shaking, "No . . . she can't be gone."

Suddenly I feel cold, almost as if the mechanism in my heart that regulates body temperature has shut down.

"This isn't right. He must have made a mistake," I force the words from my mouth, hoping to make them true. Bob must have mixed up Opal with someone else. He did say he believed so. He didn't sound too confident. Who is he anyway? He's old and probably couldn't get his facts straight if his life depended on it. Certainly he must have Alzheimer's or something like that. I bet he doesn't even know what day it is. I'm angry at myself for giving him any credit at all.

As my breathing gradually returns to normal, I gather my senses and try to think logically. Suppose she is gone, then there must be some record of it. The county clerk's office keeps death records. What about an obituary? That would give me more information than a death certificate.

If I am to take Bob's word for anything, she lived in Tustin. I should check the local library. I remember the Tustin Library keeps back issues of *The Orange County Register*. I'll prove she's alive by not finding anything. Besides it's only a five-minute drive. I start the car.

I wasn't sure what to expect when I began my investigation this morning, but this wasn't even an option. I look in the rearview mirror and see my face has become puffy. I realize tears are forming in the corners of my eyes. I didn't think I was crying, but there it is. "Stop it, she's not dead," I say aloud, "You can't go in with bloodshot eyes. People will think there's something wrong with you."

Of course, telling yourself to stop and making it happen are two separate matters altogether. The more I struggle to suppress the tears, the further I feel my heart enter uncharted territories of pain.

After pulling into the library parking lot, I put my head in my hands and rub my face vigorously, wiping away the tears, mostly, though, trying to erase the thought that she might really be gone.

I lean back in the car seat and look to my left. I'm astounded at how little the library has changed. The front is still made up of thick, heavy, brownish glass. The wooden A-frame has tan accents and hasn't been painted in several years, judging by the paint chips strewn about by the wind and lying all over the ground. The façade is sheeted with gray stucco. The red clay roof is dated but looks to be in good condition.

Walking through the doors revives the feeling from earlier this morning, the memories coming to life with startling clarity. I can't help but remember the times when we came here to study. This was my only place of refuge, where I could focus on my schoolwork and where Opal and I initially met for a legitimate purpose.

Neither of us had to study much, both being blessed with good retention skills. It was really about being with each other.

Two women are seated at the information counter—one is already helping someone else, so I turn to the other, whose name is Nancy, according to her name tag. She is younger than her co-worker, maybe in her late twenties. She is a stately looking woman with angular features and long brown hair that helps soften her otherwise hard appearance. Her disposition is casual, but she radiates self-confidence.

"Excuse me, Nancy, do you still keep records of *The Orange County Register* here?" I ask, hoping that addressing her by name will make her more inclined to help me. Everyone likes to be called by their name.

"Actually, no, sir. We stopped that practice several years ago. We do keep current newspapers for about a week, though."

"No newspaper records?" I pause. "Then how could someone look up an old obituary?"

"We don't keep those records here any longer, but our district office in Garden Grove does maintain newspaper records from the *Register*," she says, with a smile. "If that's what you're looking for?"

"I think that's what I want." I lean in closer to say in a confidential tone, "The truth is I just heard there's a possibility a friend of mine may have died and I'm looking to confirm, or . . . ," I pause. Deciding to let Nancy in further, I continue, "The girl was my first love and . . . ," I stop mid-sentence, hearing my voice beginning to waver.

Seeing the pain in my face, Nancy says, "I'll tell you what I can do. I've got a friend at the Garden Grove office. She might be able to help. I can call her."

Giving Nancy all the specifics I have on Opal—her first, middle, and last name, the city, and her parents' names—only confirms what little information I actually have. I don't have her married name, if there was one, or a date of death any more precise than three or four years ago. It's becoming apparent that leaving Bob's in such a hurry wasn't the brightest decision I have made this morning.

"This will take a few minutes."

Reaching out, she grabs my hand and gives it a sympathetic squeeze. It's comforting to feel that someone is on my side.

"Have you tried looking up the parents?" Nancy points to the section where the Yellow Pages are kept.

Why hadn't I thought of that?

It is clear that I'm not firing on all cylinders.

I walk over to the section marked "City Information" and pick up a current Tustin phone book. J, K, L, and flipping to the M section, Miller, then forward to Milton. There must be twenty different Miltons. No Stu, Stuart, or Fran Milton. A dead end. I check for Opal on the off chance she kept her maiden name, but there is no Opal Milton either. What about her brother Tim? Bingo! A match—actually three matches. I write down the three Tims' telephone numbers and addresses. I put the directory back on the shelf and find a seat to wait for Nancy.

When she gets back, she waves me over, away from her desk.

"What did you find out?" I ask, eager for her answer.

"Unfortunately, my friend Rose didn't find anything for an Opal Milton or any other person named Opal. She went back ten years and didn't find a thing. You say she was married. She probably had a different last name. Rose also tried searching for Opal's parents' names for any related articles but didn't turn up anything there either. I'm sorry."

"Thank you. Well, that's kind of good news. I mean, no obituaries and no related articles, then there's still a chance—"

"A chance . . . but not entirely true. Rose did say that newspapers no longer provide free obituaries. Meaning, if you don't pay for one, then nothing gets printed. You might be better off trying to find one of her relatives, her parents perhaps?"

I'm back to square one. After being in the detective business for all of three hours, I have only one confirmed fact: The Miltons no longer live on Livingston Street. Otherwise, all I have is the word of some old guy and the remote prospect of the three Tims. I don't relish the thought of going back to Bob's, but calling each Tim one by one and asking, "Are you the Tim with a dead sister?" doesn't appeal to me either. Bob might be the easiest way for me to get more information. But I can't bear the thought that what he said is true. I don't want it to be, and I won't believe it until I hear it directly from her family.

"I wish I could have helped you more," Nancy says with a heartfelt smile.

"Thank you again," I say and walk out the door, ready to face Bob again, and still holding on to a sliver of hope.

Thirty-three

As I return to Bob's, the day has gone from a hazy, lightly foggy morning to sun-filled and warm. I walk up to the door and knock assertively, secretly wishing that no one is home. Somehow, believing in my fantasy of the truth is better than the finality of the alternative. What if she really is gone? I have so many unanswered questions.

The door opens.

"I was hoping you would be back," Bob says, sounding relieved.

"Sorry to bother you again, but maybe you can still help me," I say. "Is there any possibility you might be wrong about Opal?"

"I'm sorry, but no. I'm positive she died several years ago," he says without hesitation.

This time I hear him.

"Then, is there anything else you can remember? Do you have a number for the Miltons? Anything?"

"Come on in and let me look." Bob waves me into the house. "To let you know, Opal was a delight," he says while leading me down the hall and into the kitchen. "She took such good care of our grandkids. She was always polite and very kind. She loved kids. You could see by the way she talked and listened to them. I know she had a couple of children herself."

I gasp. The thought breaks my heart. I look around, trying to suppress the tears.

The kitchen is crowded with knickknacks: several glass roosters, smaller pink piglet figurines, and two old-fashioned cookie jars that sit on the kitchen counter. Each jar reminds me of a character out of a Norman Rockwell painting: one is a young farmer boy in a straw hat, fishing rod in hand, and the second is a seated young girl in a simple knee-length dress holding wildflowers. Elsewhere around the room is a potpourri of cherry-designed ornaments: hand towels, pictures, and collectible plates. An assortment of empty vases clutters the windowsill—all signs of a home lived in for many years. Bob picks up a small brown address book, so overstuffed with loose papers that it no longer closes. He begins riffling through the pages, then stops, frowns, and reaches for the phone to dial a number.

"Dear, it's me again," he says. "Do we have any numbers for the Miltons? That young man is here again and I thought maybe we could help him out. I didn't find anything in the address book." He listens.

"Okay, let me check. Thanks, dear. See you tonight. Bye now."

Bob looks up and winks. He flashes a half-confident smile. "Maybe," he mutters to himself. He opens a drawer under the kitchen counter where the house phone sits. It looks to be a junk drawer. Inside are a jumble of pens, pencils, batteries, and a collection of loose papers of different colors. He extracts a packet of business cards bundled in a blue rubber band.

He shuffles through the pack like a deck of cards, then suddenly exclaims triumphantly, "Here it is," as he pulls one out. "Here's a number for Timmy's company," and hands me the card. "Please write it down."

If I hadn't been so afraid of the truth, I could have stayed here and done this in the first place. Bob gives me a piece of paper and a pen and I write down Tim's telephone number and his business address.

"Bob, thank you."

"I'm glad you came back," he says gently. "I wanted to apologize for the way I told you about Opal. I didn't mean to come out with it like that. I could tell by how quickly you left that I shocked you. I'm very sorry."

Then I feel it. She really is gone. A coolness returns to my skin. Insecurities of our past come to the forefront of my mind. There is so much I don't understand. Why didn't she call me as she promised on our last day together? Did I do something wrong to scare her away? Why didn't I just call her? I believed that somehow we would always be a part of each other's lives. Now it's all gone.

"It's okay, you didn't know," I say, holding in the emotions. "I would like to call Tim now. I should go. You've been a great help. Thank you."

Bob walks me to the door and shakes my hand once again. We exchange a few more pleasantries, and I go on my way.

* * * * * *

I DRIVE TO the church just north of Opal's old house and try to wrap my brain around the news. From where I'm parked I have a good view of the house. I don't know why, but it feels comforting to gaze at it. I like remembering the good times we spent there, together, happy. Those are some of the few times in my youth I actually have fond memories of. But today I can feel my heart breaking.

Looking around the parking lot, I see it's empty, with the exception of a sheriff's car, partially camouflaged in the back corner. The sheriff is either eating lunch or has set himself up a prime speed trap. I sit there, almost comatose, dreading to even think, to cry, to acknowledge the truth. With shaking hands, I punch Tim's number into my cell phone.

It rings twice and a man answers, identifying the company. I don't quite catch the name of it.

"Yes, I'm looking for Tim Milton," I say.

"This is he," answers the deep, gravelly voice. "May I help you?"

Is this really the same Timmy, the little boy I remember playing with Legos on the living-room floor with his brother?

"Tim, I don't know if you remember me—this is Kent Huffman. I used to date your sister."

There is a long pause, and then, "Oh yeah, I remember you," he says with a slight chuckle. "You had long blond hair—the surfer dude, right?"

"Yes, that was me. It's been a long time. I hear you're running your own business these days."

"Yeah, I started my own grading company about seven years ago. We handle mostly large grading contracts, but won't turn down smaller projects either. We can pretty much do it all. If it's dirt, we can move it."

"That's great. Listen, the reason I'm calling is I just found out about Opal. Is it true?"

"Let's see, it's been . . . what . . . she died almost ten years ago." The good cheer drains from his voice.

"Ten years ago? I was told it was only three or fours years. Ah. . . . Can you tell me what happened? I didn't get much information."

"Well, it happened in 1999. She died while giving birth. A freak thing—they say it hardly ever happens these days."

I feel empty. The birth of a child is supposed to be one of the most joyous times in a woman's life, but she died instead. I'm shocked.

"The day I got that call from Mom was one of the worst days of my life." He becomes quiet. "She's buried right there in Tustin, at the Fairhaven Memorial Park, off Fairhaven Avenue."

"Tim, I would love to see her. Would you mind if I went to visit her?"

"Sure, that would be nice. I can't believe you just found out."

"A lot has happened over the years, and we just lost contact," I lie. "I know she was married. Did she use her married name?"

"Yeah. She had recently remarried and was buried as Opal Lynn Kraft."

"Did you say remarried?" I ask, not sure if I heard him correctly.

"Yeah, it was her second. . . . Do you need directions to the cemetery?"

"No, thanks." I drop the remarriage issue. I sense he doesn't want to talk about it. "You say it's off Fairhaven. I believe that's the same place my sister was married. One last favor; can I have your parents' number?"

"You haven't spoken with them?"

"Not yet."

"I'm sure they would love to hear from you." Tim had always been like that—good-hearted. He must never have known of the turmoil I had caused the family.

I ask him for his personal number, and I thank him. Out of courtesy I give him my number, but I don't expect he will ever use it. Today might have been enough.

I'M NERVOUS ABOUT seeing the gravesite. I am only a mile or so from the cemetery, and I can feel my heart pounding fast just thinking about it. I still have to see for myself.

Thirty-four

The Fairhaven Memorial Park is not actually located in Tustin proper but on unincorporated land across the 55 Freeway, in Santa Ana. The term "park" is also misleading, as it's not exactly a place you would take your children to spend an afternoon playing on the grass and having a barbeque. The grounds are dotted with California oak, ficus, maple, and Australian carrot-wood trees, and enclosed by a wrought-iron fence, giving the cemetery a peaceful ambiance. The grass is kept short, cut every Wednesday after the previous week's flowers have been removed. A small stone church lies within the park's sixty-nine acres and is often used for weddings and other occasions, as well as funerals.

This is where Sissy and Phil were married the summer after I last saw Opal. Phil, a.k.a. Skunk, kept his word, and soon after the wedding, they moved to the woods of Sisters,

Oregon. Yes, my sister Sissy lives in Sisters—pretty ironic. They have two children of their own. I would never have dreamed this is where Opal would eventually be laid to rest.

I stop at the information center to find out where she is buried. They give me a map pinpointing the site, and I follow it until I spot the marking A23 painted in black on the curb. I pull over and park. Quickly looking around, I think, *Gee, there must be over 280 plots in this one section alone.*

As I get out of the car, I feel the sun beating down on my forehead. It's now warm with no wind to speak of. I approach her gravesite and the coldness returns, but this time the chill goes through my entire body, shaking me to the core.

Opal's marker is unpretentious—made of black marble with a sleeping angel engraved on the upper left hand corner. It reads simply:

OPAL LYNN KRAFT
1960–1999
OUR BELOVED MOTHER, WIFE, DAUGHTER,
SISTER, GRANDCHILD, TEACHER,
FRIEND AND ANGEL.

As I kneel next to the headstone, my eyes fill with tears. For the first time today, I let them go, no longer wanting to resist.

"Why did I wait so long?" I vent. "Why didn't you call? I did my part. I broke up with Diana the next day. Why didn't you? What about your promises?"

Addressing the headstone, I go on, more angrily, "Why did you die? Look at the mess you left behind." The tears continue to roll down my cheeks.

My cell phone rings. Wiping away the tears with the hem of my shirt, I have an overwhelming intuition that I should answer. I clear my throat.

"Hello, this is Kent," I say shakily.

"Hi, Kent. This is Mrs. Milton. Tim called me and said you wanted to speak with me." Her voice has not aged, and is as emotionless as I remember. I never could read her true feelings.

"Yes, my god, it's been a long time," I say, surprised. Unsure exactly how to broach the subject, I blurt, "I just found out about Opal. I'm so sorry."

"It's okay now," Mother Milton says calmly. "She's no longer my child. She's with God now."

"Do you think we could meet?" I ask. "I would love to see you. I'll be happy to meet you at your house."

"I would like to see you too," she replies, "but not at my house today. We're getting ready to go camping and things are a little untidy. And I don't have a lot of time. Where are you now?"

"I'm at the cemetery."

"Oh, my. . . . I live five minutes away. I'll meet you there," she says, sounding somewhat put out, as if I have encroached on her turf. "Bye." And she abruptly hangs up.

OVER THE NEXT few minutes I feel like I'm waiting for a dentist appointment; I know why I'm there, but I'm not exactly sure what's going to happen. I try to look everywhere except at the headstone. The shrubs are growing wild between the bars of the black, wrought-iron fence. On the adjacent lawn, a large, forest-green canopy has been set up for a funeral. Six folding chairs sit on a patch of artificial grass; behind them, the mound of dirt that will fill the open grave. The scent from the multitude of freshly cut flowers fills the air. I can't bear to look down at the headstone. If I think of her, I will start to cry again, and I don't want Mother Milton to see me bawling like a baby. Perhaps I perceive myself more as a tough guy, and everyone knows real men don't cry. What a load of shit that is. Opal was right about me. I am a teddy bear on the inside.

As I watch the road, a lemon-yellow pickup truck comes into view and parks behind my Jaguar. A woman gets out and grabs a bouquet before closing the door. She is an older woman, slim and in good condition for her age. As she comes nearer, I can see more clearly the passage of time in her face, as I am sure she sees it in mine. Deep lines mark her forehead, and when she removes her sunglasses, crow's feet and other wrinkles are revealed.

She smiles and says, "How are you?" as she places a bouquet of tiger lilies on the grave. They appear to be from her garden because they have already begun to wilt.

"I'm good," I say, and give her a hug. "I'm so sorry."

She feels bony and extremely stiff, almost as if she doesn't want to touch me.

"Kent, she's been gone a long time now," she says gently.

"Yes, but not for me," I reply, wanting her to understand my feelings. "Please, can you tell me about it?"

"Let's get out of the sun," she says as we move some ten yards off, into the ample shade of a maple tree.

"The baby was her third," she says. "Earlier that week, September first—it was a Wednesday—we spent the whole day together. We talked about everything—the C-section, scheduled for Friday, how she already missed her students. Did you know she was a teacher?"

"No, I didn't know. But, it doesn't surprise me either. She always loved children and had told me she wanted to be a teacher."

"She taught first grade, and she loved it. Opal wanted to go back to work as soon as she could after having the baby. I told her to wait and see. That maybe she'd feel differently once the baby was born. But she was sure she would. We had a good day together, just mother and daughter.

"Then, on Friday, Opal went into the hospital as planned. She wasn't feeling well in the morning, though. Apart from her brothers, most of the family was there. Mack, her husband, was so excited about the new baby. But something went wrong. There were complications and she passed away at noon—or one—I don't remember exactly, but I know it was right on the hour. They said amniotic fluid got into her bloodstream, and she died instantly. Her son, Michael, survived. He's nine now, ten soon."

As I listen to her tell the story, I still can't read her. She betrays no emotion—nothing. There's not even the slightest quiver in her voice.

"Gosh, it must have been devastating," I say. "I'm stunned." I feel my nose begin to sting and know the tears will soon follow.

"It was difficult for everyone, but especially for her two children from her first marriage, and it goes without saying, her new husband. They had only been married a short time, less than a year. Everything happened so fast."

"So she was married before?" I ask, wanting to satisfy my curiosity.

"Yes, but that's another story. It almost didn't happen."

"What do you mean?"

"Well. . . . On the day of the wedding, she wasn't sure if she wanted to go through with it. She kept babbling on about something with her best friend Sandy, though I never did find out about what. She fidgeted around a lot, not wanting to come out of her room. After an hour of waiting, I finally had to step in. Fortunately, reason prevailed. It was chaos." She pauses, as if this is a memory she does not care to relive. "She had two beautiful children, Kristina, who is now in college, and Patrick, who's a senior at Tustin High."

"Did you know she came to see me a couple weeks before the wedding?"

"No, I didn't know that."

I'm not sure whether to believe her. I can see the wheels turning in her head, but then she grimaces. She knows.

I decide to let the matter drop.

"Was she happy?" I ask.

"In the end, she was. I think she found what she was looking for."

"I know Opal was confused at times. I felt she was always searching for something." The moment I say it, I regret it. Here I am telling a mother about her daughter, someone I haven't seen in twenty-seven years. I have no right. I lost that right many years ago. But deep down I have to ask myself if I'm still angry at this woman, after all these years, for all that she took from me, and from Opal. I wonder if it ever crosses her mind that if she had only let us be together, Opal might be alive today.

"I liked her better as an adult," Mother Milton says finally.

Ouch. That cuts me to the bone. I know she always disapproved of us as a couple and viewed our relationship as some unhealthy, youthful obsession. I manage to hold my tongue.

"Tell me, Kent. Why are you here?" Mother Milton asks, more sharply now.

"I just wanted to find Opal and ask her how her life was going. Is she happy, that sort of thing. I had no other agenda." I am instinctively defensive. "I'm happily married, and have been for nineteen years. We have two children, and I'm recently retired, so I had the time."

"Aren't you a little young to retire?" She looks confused.

"Sure, but we've worked hard and made some good financial decisions. It's afforded me the one luxury you can never have enough of—time. Time to be with my children and experience their growing years, something I never got from my parents. Also, time to find those from my past who were special to me. Over the years, I've lost contact with so many. I wanted to see how their lives have unfolded. And Opal was uppermost in my mind. I hoped to catch up with her, tell her of my life, let her know I think of her occasionally, and sincerely wish her the best in life. . . ." I trail off and turn away, tearing up at the thought that none of this will ever happen.

I don't tell Mother Milton of my haunting dreams, or about the painting's eerie likeness, and I certainly don't reveal that I wanted to ask Opal why she never came back to me.

"Losing my brother spurred me on," I say, turning back to face her.

"What happened to him?" she asks, softening.

"Danny died. It must have been about six months after Opal. Of sleep apnea."

"No." She looks surprised.

"He was diagnosed a couple of years earlier—went to bed, turned on his breathing apparatus, fell asleep, and died. He forgot to put the mask on. They found it in his hand."

"How unfortunate," she says. "But I'm sure he's with God, like my good little girl."

I don't know how to react other than to nod in agreement.

"How is the rest of your family? Is your mom still married to that same man?" She asks.

"Yes, of course. Mom and Bernie have been married now for—what—thirty-plus years. Both retired and pretty much keep to themselves." I'm not about to tell her any of the lies and manipulation Mom perpetrated over the years. Our relationship is all but over. Apart from the occasional birthday card, we have no contact. We simply see life differently.

"What about your father?" She continues to probe.

"You mean Wes? I haven't seen him since Danny's funeral. We never saw eye-to-eye, as you know." I leave out the fact that he isn't my real father and that he died a lonely, bitter man. "And your family?"

"We have ten grandchildren," she says proudly. "And, by God's grace, we expect our first great-grandchild later this year. And Opal's little boy is such a handsome young man."

"Do you have pictures of them?"

"Not with me," she says.

I don't believe her. What proud grandmother doesn't carry pictures?

"When you have the time," I say, "I would love to see some pictures of Opal in her later years."

"That can be done. Oh, we have some old pictures of you wearing a blue tux. Blue must be your favorite color. Look what you're wearing today, a light blue shirt. And is that your blue Jaguar?"

"Yes, it is." I say, feeling the tension ease. "Do you think I could call you next week, after you get back from camping? Maybe meet for lunch? I would love to hear more about her life."

"Sounds wonderful," she says, not unkindly.

We hug, say our goodbyes and she leaves me there. She doesn't look back at Opal's headstone, or wave to me. With her back straight and rigid, she drives off, stone-faced.

I walk back to the grave, kneel, and shed a few tears.

Epilogue

Chasing the memories away . . .

I'm back at her grave. I've been here quite often since that day, probably much more than I should. I no longer have dreams of her, am no longer haunted by our past, or in need of answers. The painting has been removed from the office and has found a new place in the attic. I'm not ready to dispose of it altogether, but I will someday.

As for Mrs. Milton, she never returned any of my calls. I realize I must represent a hurt that can't be healed and is best left unaddressed. I understand.

For today, it's time to say goodbye. I kneel down next to her headstone and pull a piece of paper from my front pocket. It's something I copied down earlier in the morning—part of a song, our song, the one we shared in the beginning.

I don't read its lyrics or even unfold the paper. The words have inherited a different meaning from the one they had when we first listened to them. Instead, I place the paper on the grass next to the one white rose I had brought.

"Opal, you will always be my Disney girl, the fantasy of my youth, and hold a special place in my heart. You were my first love, and I will always love you that way. But I've come to say goodbye. I will miss you. Even more, I will miss the thought of you."

I open my left hand, revealing a golden ring. I had taken it from my memory box. I lay it on the headstone, below the engraved angel. The ring is modest, but still shines like the day I bought it . . . oh, so many years ago. I had wanted her to be mine, but she was not. The gold band has gone unused, its purpose incomplete, unfulfilled.

Speaking aloud again, "This ring is yours and always has been . . . and here it shall stay, with you.

"So, Opal, what a journey this has been. The one question I wanted answered will remain unanswered, but it has been resolved. You know, 'What if?' You see, the decision you made by not choosing me, regardless of your reasons, has made me the man I am. Your decision changed my life.

"I had always assumed I was the one having a major impact on your life, influencing how you thought, things you'd say, your world view. But the truth is that you changed my life more than I ever affected yours. Because of your decision, I am happy. I have a good life, a wonderful wife, and two terrific children. I met her about a year after we last saw each other. For all of this, I thank you.

"The many questions, and the answers to them, no longer seem so important.

"I will always treasure the memories we created together, the good and the bad times. Although today it's mostly the good memories that remain. We revealed our souls to each other. The emotions were indeed very intense, but at that age, everything was more luminous, enhanced just by virtue of being new. We experienced the tenderness of touch, the sharing of raw emotions, and the wonders of first love. So many firsts.

"And who doesn't remember their first love?

"I only hope you had a good life. My biggest sorrow is not for me but for your family. Your children were left without a mother, and that's irreplaceable. I empathize with the heartache they must have felt and feel even today.

"Ultimately, though, I needed to listen. The dreams were a message. I believe in my heart it was you, giving me a sign, and I ignored it for years. I should have tried to find you earlier. The lesson I've learned, and need to share, is that if anyone has ever had someone special in their life—a past love or a close friend they haven't seen in a while—find them—don't wait—because sometimes it's too late. In my case, it was."

With my right fist I tap my heart three times and point to her headstone. I get up and start to walk off, then turn and say in a soft whisper, "Goodbye, my Disney girl."